I0732843

curious women
and other creatures

Sam Le Butt

curious women

and other creatures

Radical Bookshop and Press
4838 Richard Road SW, Suite 300
Calgary, AB T3E 6L1
Canada

FIC029000 - Fiction, Short Stories

Editors: Lexie Angelo
Cover Design: Sam Le Butt

Typeset in Bookmania

ISBN-13: 978-1-990201-00-4

Printed in the United Kingdom

For the creatures, curious all

contents

Waking with the birds 9

Birthday 15

Carlyon Babe 21

Hot and Bothered 43

The Root Cause 51

Julie's Place 57

Washed Up 85

The Endling 113

Acknowledgements

About the Author

WAKING WITH THE BIRDS

I woke up this morning with a nest of baby birds in my mouth. Prodded awake by the smoky fingers of dawn, I lay on my back with my lips still gummy from sleep, my blanket twisted and damp with sweat. *Must have been dreaming again.*

I opened my mouth to yawn and heard the delicate cheeping. Scrambling up off the floor, I moved to the mirror-shard on the earthen wall. I opened my mouth and saw them there: four sickly looking things, writhing bald on my tongue. Each about the size of a peanut, they were still young, and still lacking the black feathers I had seen in the murals—but they had a strong song. It was loud and stirred something deep in my shoulders. I flexed my arms and I tried to sing along, but each roll of my tongue heaved them around, and they wailed plaintively. I closed my mouth. I would have to keep this quiet, at least in the towers. Who knows who might try and snatch them, claim them as their own? If Rail found out, he would swipe them for sure, the dirty sneak. I would take them straight to G-ma. She would protect them. She'd know what to do.

I kept my chin held high and my head level, trying not to disturb the nest. I left my little stone chamber through the large exit draped in cloth, draw-stringing it shut behind me. I weaved through the tunnels, crouching down low. The twins Moa and Dodo went flying by, but I had no voice to tell them to slow down. *You'll bowl someone over!* They never listen to me anyway, although Mother Takahe says my whiney chirrups will deepen into respectful calls of authority soon enough. I passed the long-empty nursery, then doubled back, feeling my way along the cool, dusty walls, and used its sky-hole to shortcut into the main slide.

This was a mistake. The main slide functioned like an artery, with countless other smaller tunnels feeding into and cutting across it. Workers and runners shot across my path with stern, sharp cries of warning, and I clawed at the smooth surface to slow my descent. I emerged at the bottom of the stone tower into the blistering sun of the street wide-eyed and breathless. I opened my mouth to get some air to the birds and drain the gathering saliva back down my throat. They cheeped appreciatively.

Keeping my dry lips ever so slightly parted, I began to shuffle cautiously through the market. Everyone was still setting up, but freshly roasted crickets hooked me by the nostrils and dragged me closer, up on the tips of my toes, nails skimming the small rocks and dents of the sandstone road. The vendor Ol' Kioea greeted me from behind his stand.

"Good morning my little Laughing Owl; you're up early on this skin-rippingly hot morning! What brings you out from the cool so soon?"

I eyed Ol' Kioea, wondering whether he could be trusted. He was a gossip, but also a true believer. At dusk, his song was always one of the loudest. He might be able to help. I tipped my head back and mouthed around the little creatures, "Ah ha' a mao-hul o 'irds!"

"What? Speak up gal."

I tried again. "Ah wo'e ah iss 'ornin wi' a mao-hul o 'irrrdds!" I pointed frantically into my mouth.

He turned back to his insects. "Ehhh, I can't understand a thing you chicks say these days. Could be chirping a dead tongue for all I know. Run along, little Laughing Owl!"

I hesitated. The smell of the barbecue was exciting the birds; their sharp beaks grazed the inside of my cheeks. Ol' Kioea started to whistle. I plucked a smoking cricket from the spit and stuffed it in my pocket. I turned and hurried away. After all, I had mouths to feed! Let alone my own. *How would I eat with a mouth full of birds?* G-ma would show me how. She knew everything there was to know about birds. She would help me not to repeat the mistakes of the past.

I inched my way across town, dipping from shade to shade. Those out and about early called to me, but I slipped past them with cheeks puffed out and a half-hearted wave. I kept the arches of my feet high, high-stepping with only the hardened skin of the balls of my feet touching the ground, like Mother Takahe had taught us runners ("Like the majestic ostrich once did!" Mother Takahe had hopped around the sweating, mud-walled classroom in example). It was a long way to the next settlement over the scorched plains, and I had to protect my feet ("Especially since our wings have burnt away!" She had rapped on my shoulder blades.)

I hopped past graffiti covering the high stone walls—the mural painted after the Great Flight now had a giant man added to the familiar scene, his mouth a gaping hole into which the flock of little black birds flew. It was the work of the radical Mantas, who believed it was all our fault.

I made it to the other side of town, my neck aching from keeping my head tipped back—a hard thing to do when you're trying not to draw attention to yourself. The cheeping had quieted, and I hurried as fast as I could. When I reached the old water tower, it took my eyes a minute or so to adjust to the cool shadows. Little Bulbul was there, glinting impishly in the dark. He had been relieved years ago, when it was clear they weren't coming back, but I don't think he can take the heat anymore. So, he just huddled here in the dark, trying to swindle a few coins out of G-ma's visitors. What he spent them on was anyone's guess.

I was in a hurry and pressed my forehead to his. I could smell his little meaty breaths. Mother Takahe said it was important to respect the Augury, although few people I knew still had faith in its use. She believed the Great Flight was just a migration, and the birds would return once more, rising from the opposite horizon with all they had taken with them ("All we can do now is show them we

11

have changed." She had pulled my arms outstretched to the sides, almost yanking them from their sockets and lifting my chin to the sky.)

Little Bulbul waited for the accompanying incantation, but I couldn't say it on account of my mouthful, and he flipped his supple, brown palm up into my face for a donation.

"Ah 'orry Hi-hul 'ul-'ul, ah ha' a moa-hul o 'irds!"

He grunted and thrust his little leather hand higher. How was I going to reach G-ma at the top if I couldn't pay the stupid doorman? Behind him, in the softly illuminated chute, I saw the rope hanging there. I pushed past the little old man and grabbed the running line, calling down to him some garbled apology as I ascended the narrow shaft to the top of the tower. I was nearly at the top when a hand gripped my wrist.

I looked up into G-ma's wrinkled face. She pulled me forward—a little roughly—and I tripped off the ledge and onto the dusty roof of the Augury. I steadied myself as she shuffled to the edge to look out over the wall. *She must be boiling in all those layers.*

I moved slowly to her side, panting from the rush, my little wards shuffling around on my tongue to balance themselves in the wind of my breath. I peeked at the view from my awkward, head-tilted position. Cobalt met by a fat slab of brown. The aching desert plains, crawling with bugs unfettered from their flying predators. The Mantas claim all this used to be water, but Mother Takahe says we have to look up, not down. Forward, not back.

G-ma stood scanning the bleached blue, her little black eyes screwed up tight against the glare. Turning up to her, I opened my mouth and let the birds do the explaining. She lifted her tiny, stick-like hands from underneath her robes and pushed up her thick, woven sleeves, before clamping her hands on either side of my face. They were strong for such spindly twigs. She peered into my mouth. Face tilted back, I tried to look up, away from her bulbs of strong, white hair; it seemed rude to stare at them this close. Opened up to the air, the birds wobbled on my tongue, their tiny claws gripping harder, making my eyes water. They seemed to be drawn to her, like she was their true mother.

12

"Ahhh," G-ma sighed, a huge smile propping up the tanned folds of her face. "I haven't heard that sound for a hundred years."

She tilted my face down so she was looking into my eyes. With her hard, hook nose and raisin eyes, she really did look like a bird. Maybe all these years spent searching for them had willed her features to comply. She spoke to me very softly. "You must look after these birds, little Laughing Owl. This is the sign I have been waiting for."

BIRTHDAY

"Nervous?" Some friend-of-a-friend hovers in the hall. I stand with one finger jammed onto the 'Close' button, my other hand on my waist. He's the last to leave and he's really not getting it.

"No Yun, I think I can handle it."

He snorts. "Oh my god, after the year you've had? I'd be shitting myself!" He wriggles his face forward, the door smushing his cheeks together. "I mean, you lost your birthmammy, your partner, not to mention that whole 'position shake-up', and it's not like you handled the whole thing with quiet dignity and—"

"Bye Yun." I push his forehead out of the door's grip and it seals shut. His little voice pipes up through the glass.

"I'm actually just kidding, but if you do want me to come back afterwards with a batch of roasted-botanical iced gin-pops—"

"You can shove each of them into your overly-weathered arsehole," I yell through the door. "It could use some soothing."

I stalk down the hallway, picking up empty glasses, cigarette ends, and the wrinkled skins of popped balloons as I go. Yun. Who even is Yun? He only wants to come back to gawk at the fresh product. I stop and take a deep breath. It's half an hour until midnight, and I have to pull myself together before the big appointment.

Apart from the lack of people, the kitchen is still well in party mode. Dark and pulsing, the shadows slime up and down the walls like chemmed-up funk-whores. Nah, they've all gone! I laugh maniacally as I flick off the strobes and finger-stop the spinning disco balls and plug the champagne fountain. Well, sparkling wine. Cut-backs were made. The darkness groans from the bright light, just like my recent guests when I requested that they all get out. Yun said I should do a dramatic reveal, but I want to be alone for this. I begin covering the many mirrors crowded into my small, hot living room.

After I'd announced the end of the festivities, my good-time galpal Voonda had dragged me from the dancefloor (the sliver of space between the divan and the drinks cabinet) to the kitchen. "Are you sure you wanna do this by yourself?" she had asked. "My last change was pretty brutal—who knew you could see the effects of moving house in your knees! It really helped having someone there."

"Having June there," I pointed out.

"Well, anyone." She shrugged, raising her eyebrows along with her arms. She was dressed only in glitter, with a smoking bird's-nest up-do.

"Well, I don't have Zara with me this year, do I?" I leaned down and zooped a white line from the kitchen counter.

"No, I know. But I can be here if you need me to be. It can be pretty harrowing, to see it all in one go. Especially at this age and especially...y'know..." I looked up at her. "At this speed," she finished diplomatically. I tusked and bent over the counter again. "C'mon, you need someone here to stop that little voice in your head."

"It's not the voice in my head I'm worried about," I replied, straightening.

"At least let me help you cover the mirrors. There are so many, it'll take ages."

I exhaled, putting the straw down. "Nah, I wanna do it all by myself. I need some one-on-one time. Just me-myself-and-I." Voonda nodded in time with the strobe. "Oh god," I said, putting my head in my hands. "She is gonna have a field day this year."

Voonda clicked in agreement. "The person looking back at you can be pretty harsh. Partly what we're paying for though, eh? That little pep-talk." She reached out and rubbed my earlobe. "Call me afterwards if you need anything."

"It'll be okay," I sniffed and rubbed a finger beneath my leaking nostril. "Everything that's happened this year, it's for the best anyway. I could use some time out of the management game to sort my head out, it was so much *pressure*. And Zara will be busy downloading all her bullshit onto her new, state-of-the-art fuckdoll—I mean, girlfriend."

Voonda giggled behind a powdered hand.

"And I have all of the time in the world to take care of her wretched iguana whilst she moves the rest of her stuff out." We both glanced over at Gerard on his high perch in the corner, eyes swivelling round like centrifuges.

"Hopefully those lights don't completely ruin his brain." I let out a skin-piercing shriek when Voonda slapped my arm. My toned, brown arm. I wonder how much skin would sag this year. Then Voonda dragged me back onto the dancefloor, moving behind me and lifting my arms above my head. I laughed, and my friends all gathered round, each holding a mirror up to me. My last chance to bask.

Later, after everyone has left, I light a cigarette by the window, shivering in my tiny dress. It had been a good party, and badly needed. Everyone else may be shimmering down the Five-Year-Plan catwalk, but here in Readjustment Alley we have a good time too. I take a drag and look out over the unending city. Feral dogs howl and I tip my head back to howl right along with them. Feels good to be part of the night-chorus—I've become a full-time member since Zara left. Her eyes had glowed coward-yellow when she told me she couldn't do it anymore.

"I need to be with someone who's comfortable with who they are," she'd said.

"You mean someone who can afford to get permanent adjustments?" I had spat back.

"Ocean is just naturally very... happy with how she looks," she had smiled, self-satisfaction radiating off her like a serotonin glow lamp.

I take another drag. Well, I hope she's happy with her choices. I'm happy with mine. In the corner, Gerard is slumped over. Hopefully he's dead, and I won't have to suffer those rotating eyes of scrutiny every morning before my coffee.

I look at the clock. Ten to midnight.

The appointment on my last birthday hadn't been so rough, but then I had been teetering atop that elusive wave of skin-to-skin intimacy, on top of a recent promotion. That apophatic strategy pitch that had finally but decisively pierced the tired skin of the markets. What a year that had been. I watch the smoke curl out of the window. Mum had been slowly withering even then, crutch-propped at the launch party, but I hadn't noticed. Blinded by the whirling mirage of Zara and her jewelled smile. Hadn't clocked Mum's nibbling illness until it was too late. That's the mirror for you though. It hides it all until it's too late. She died soon after her 67th birthday—probably best that she only had to live with that sunken skeleton for a few weeks.

I close the window and walk to my bedroom, instinctively glancing in the hall mirror, only to be met with black cloth. Voonda said it was best to ease it in, uncovering maybe just one mirror a day in the coming weeks. Give me a chance to feel at home before *looking* at home. I undress, gazing down at this year's bod one final time. What have I put you through? All those carefully administered benders, all that medicinal cocaine. The alarm goes off and I walk to the bathroom. Wouldn't wanna miss the show.

I position myself in front of the mirror, starkers. Why did I choose this? Why delay the inevitable? And it's only gonna get worse from now on. I hold my chin up. Come on now. It's just like ripping off a plaster.

I stand cryogenically-still, fists clenched, staring straight at myself, eyes ablaze. I watch as small lines fold around them, streak by my mouth. I see my neck sag. I watch as hues flash across my skin, hair working its natural path along my upper lip at time-capture speed. I watch my nipples pucker slightly and then my breasts drop a few centimetres lower. It's all so small, but to see a year's worth in a minute is hard to watch. A permanent frown line carves its way into the centre of my forehead. The worry, the paranoia, the drinking when she fucked off; to fuck her. I raise my hand slowly to stroke the bleaching of grey in my black hair—finger a silvery strand of grief. Like mum's hair weaved into mine.

It's over soon enough and the result is there. The new me. Still Suzi. Just a bit... shitter. I push my face up close to the glass, raking my fingers through the new lines. I smush my cheeks round to inspect every chip, every sign of damage. Take a step back, lift a hand to my waist and turn from side to side. It's actually not that bad! I grin. Considering my average blood-toxicity level this year, this is pretty good. "Apart from you two," I coo to my breasts, cupping one in each hand. "You've taken a real hit this year, gals." I let them swing back down to their new level. "Well," I say to the reflection in the mirror, "maybe I should get everyone back over, eh? Celebrate the jammiest age-up this side of the millennium, ha!" I lean off the cold edge of the sink and move towards the door. I check my phone. The messages are already pouring in. "Yes Yun, you can return!" I read aloud whilst typing.

"Ah-ah-ah," says the creamy mirror-voice. "Where do you think you're going?"

I whip round, eyes narrowing. "Excuse me?"

The woman in the mirror looks at me with candied eyes. "You think that was it? Oh baby, we haven't even started."

CARLYON BABE

At dawn, the beach was nearly empty; just a few brave surfers dotted amongst the froth, being tossed about like salad. The sunrise loitered beneath the horizon, occasionally probing the sealine with a long, bright finger, pink from the cold. On the beach, a dog and his walker moved slow against the wind. Later, the beach would be overrun with tourists drenched in ice cream, wrestling with windbreaks.

A fishing boat approached the shore, though these were not fishing grounds. You had to go further west or south coast to catch anything these days. Couple quays down there were covered with a fine sheen of scales, and you could buy mackerel baps that still wriggled. Yet here she was (because boats are all shes, and so is the sea) steaming ahead at quite a speed. Behind her salted window screen there was a lined, brown face haloed by a mane of soft, grey hair. The corners of his beard-mouth were stained rollie-yellow.

Mark Towen had been smoking since he was eleven and would probably live until he was ninety because sometimes smokers do live that long. He had been working boats since about the same time, but he had never had a catch like today. His leathery hands were clamped on the wheel tight, and his eyes—more-watery-than-land-working eyes—were strained open wide as he hurtled towards the beach. The surfers yelled as he thundered through their designated area and up onto the beach.

The boat came to a stop, wedged in the sand, foam churning around her. Mark didn't move. He couldn't turn round and face what he had dragged up from the seabed. Bad luck was what he had dragged up. He had beached Belle in a panic, his livelihood. And now he didn't know what to do. Maybe if he stayed with his back to it, he could just watch the day at the beach, and nothing would be different.

Ray Thompson was also out early that morning. He liked to stroll along the beach before the emmets transformed it into a singular writhing organism. The way he saw it, you need less sleep when you're old, as you're about to have a nice long nap anyway, and before you go it's nice to see the sunrise, especially coming up from the sea. He drifted across the beach like a shell in the current, and it took a moment or two for him to process the sudden intrusion of a boat named Belle onto the scene before him.

He eyed the vessel. Round here, you were more likely to catch a nasty infection than a fish. Ray knew caravanning did not mean what it did in his day, with your aunts and sisters all playing cards whilst the rain poured on the sand outside. However, unlike most locals, Ray didn't mind this new teenaged crowd; in fact, he half-wished he could join in. Nina wouldn't like it though. His wife was an imposing walrus of a woman, and the local authority on every happening in town, big or small. She found the unpredictability of these new caravanners extremely unsettling, their behaviour beyond her sphere of influence.

So, Ray would watch them, night after night, from his post outside The King's Arms, away from the judging eyes of his wife, with a quarter-full pint glass of still brown ale in one hand. As those fluorescent bodies whirled by, he would feel a faint light echoing weakly within the murk of his mind, and, resisting the urge to follow the procession, he would potter back inside to bore his fellow bar flies with the story of the great lost love of his youth. Nina didn't like this either.

His wife's scolding replayed through his mind as Ray hurried down to the water's edge, arms up like a toddler keeping its balance. He stopped short of the prow and, looking up into the salted glass of the windscreen, could just make out the ghostly face of a fisherman.

He called up. "What you doing slamming into the beach like that?"

Mark Towen stayed staring straight ahead.

"Boats are menna be on the sea," said Ray, raising his eyebrows.

Mark turned down to the rumpled old man. "Don't you think I know that?" he said, voice all throat and flake. "But if you'd seen what I got on back, you'd be frozen stiff as me." He backed out from the standing shelter and Ray followed him along the side to the stern, where Mark let down the ladder. Ray almost had a good laugh because his joints could barely carry him horizontally, let alone vertically up a small, metal ladder, but the fisherman was looking down at something on the deck so intently, with such a troubled look on his face, that Ray set to wrenching himself up.

At first, it looked like any other mound of dead mackerel, mottle-backed and silver-bellied.

But then they moved as one and Ray saw her, shiny as a morning star. He stumbled and had to grip the side. Sure, her head was smooth and bald, and her tits were hard and scaly. But there was no doubt.

A mermaid.

And she was out cold.

"Jesus Christ," Ray breathed. He turned to Mark. "You know it's bad luck to have a bird on board."

"That ain't no bird," said Mark, his fingers working out a cigarette from damp baccy. "Easterly swept me up and I must've caught her in the swell. This is bad luck, right bad luck. We gotta put her back."

Ray crouched down before the coiled creature and peered up close to her face. From within the murk of his mind that faint light throbbed brighter. He reached out a white, wizened hand and whispered into the salty dawn: "Could it really be you?"

He watched as two black eyes unfolded wetly like sea anemones.

Then she was batting away his hand and flinging herself across the deck with an ancient cry of some strange sea language.

The men screamed and drew together. Against the far side, the mermaid writhed around in the fluorescent green netting, getting more and more entangled with each thwack of her massive tail. A constant stream of exotic sounds poured from her mouth. And then: "Let me out! Let me the fuck out!"

Mark's ciggie hung from his bottom lip, fluttering in the wind. He nudged Ray with his elbow. "Bit of a mouth on this one."

Ray wasn't listening. He was staring at the wriggling temptress. It was her. It had to be.

Mark took a tentative step forward. "O' glorious and wrathful daughter of the sea—" he began.

"Cut that shit out," said the mermaid. She had stopped her thrashing, well and truly bound.

Mark cleared his throat. "I just wanna make it clear that I had no intention of wresting you away from your, your majestic kingdom beneath the waves, and that neither you, nor any of your sacred kin-folk—"

The mermaid coughed.

Mark pulled a hand through his mane. "I just mean to say, please pass my, er, respects, along to your council of elders—"

She sucked in her large globular eyes.

"—or king—"

Letting out a seal's bark, her eyes emerging again with a pop.

"Whoever's in charge down there," Mark waved his hands. "I meant no harm."

A seagull cut a screeching silhouette above them. The mermaid watched as the siren continued its inland. "It's not down there I'm worried about."

Mark looked to Ray, but he just stood there, gawping.

"Y'alright, mate?" He tailed off when he saw tears streaming down Ray's face.

"Fifty years," Ray whispered.

The mermaid tucked her chin. "Excuse me?"

Ray chuckled wetly. "She were my bird backalong." Sure, she swore like a sailor, and he tried not to look at the shiny scalp or the stony nipples because he *knew* this was the same beguiling vixen who had lured him into Hawker's Bay all those years ago. The boys at The King's weren't gonna believe this!

On the beach around the boat, more people had begun to appear: the owners of the beach front cafes, and the lifeguards, finally. Their van trundled down the sand, stopped, and out jumped two healthy, tanned boys with white teeth and white souls. They could have been twins. They approached the boat.

"What's going on up there?" shouted Jack. The more chiselled of the two, he had only moved down West when he was twelve and his lean, Home County accent had resisted any sanding. He swung around the ladder and hoisted himself up to peer on deck. Mark and Ray turned with bent knees and that face men wear when they have been caught doing something they're really not supposed to be, yet are still furious at the interruption.

Jack didn't notice either of them. "Holy shit man."

His partner Henry, a little doughier, especially in the nose, called up from the beach. "What?" Jack pulled out his phone and started recording. The mermaid put her hands up. "Hey, get that thing out my face." Jack let out a clean, sharp laugh. "It's some kinda fucked-up mermaid, dude!"

Within an hour of Jack posting the video, the beach was packed. It would be busy on a day like this anyway, but a mermaid on top of that? Queues running out the car park. They had even managed to dredge up a few policemen, rusty from underuse.

Ian Prynn, Chief Constable (Cuntstable, if you read the fingered message in his van dust), stood around with his crew, hands tucked into the peck-pockets of his hi-vis vest. Every now and then he removed his too-large helmet and gave his receding hairline a good scratch. They had tried to create a 'police cordon,' as they had seen on telly at the protests upcountry, but it was hard to make a ring around a boat with only three men.

Locals pushed their way through the crowd of tourists to stand at their rightful place at the front. Their beach: their mermaid—even if she wasn't quite what the local cafe signs said she would be. Amongst them appeared Jean and Spence, her with red spiky hair above a downturned mouth, him with a belly as big as a barrel. It was funny to see his shins kicking out from beneath it when he came careering down the sand, but then not so funny to look up and see his open maw contorted with grief, and even less funny to remember he lost his daughter at sea a year ago.

"Is it her? Is it?" He almost bowled over the Chief.

Ian bunched his hands up on Spence's fleeced shoulders. "Spence, mate, Spence. It's not her."

Spence spat. "Who then?"

Ian leaned close; raised his eyebrows. "No one local."

There was a chorus of beeps up on the sandy cliff-top road as the TV station arrived, pushing through the queue of cars. With the van still in motion, the side door opened, and Chloe Wellington's blonde hair snaked out with the wind, as though dragged by some invisible hand. She was interning at the station and covering for that shiny-toothed Simon Porter whilst he was off conducting 'important investigative journalism concerning current Britain-EU relations' in the club strips of southern Spain. Chloe wasn't going to mess up this opportunity.

"Piran!" she screamed behind her as she waddled down the slipway in her tight skirt. "Bring the drone! I'm not missing a single detail up on that boat!" She positioned herself in front of the growing crowd, plastering down her hair, swapping the paw-like microphone back and forth. Piran set down the camera and held up a three, two, one.

26

"Good morning Cornwall. You're here with Chloe Wellington, bringing you breaking news from the North Coast. In his indefatigable—"

Piran sliced his hand across his throat.

"—Tireless quest to feed the nation, one of our local boys has caught more than he bargained for this morning: a mermaid, ladies and gentlemen, an actual, real-life mermaid. The stories are true, and you heard it here first – stay tuned for exclusive footage of this exotic guest as she makes her way into our country, and, no doubt, our hearts, at this trying time of continental tension..."

Back up on deck, the mermaid squirmed from Ray and his soft, mulchy eyes.

"My sweet Morveren, it's been so long." His arms floundered round the figure of Mark, who knelt before her cutting holes in the net. "You sung to me a song of purest honey, calling me down from that blasted boat—"

"Keep him away from me," said the mermaid to Mark, batting away one of Ray's prying fingers. Mark looked at her, and in her bulbous eyes he caught twin images of dark waves curling, beckoning talons of the unfathomable depths. Every storm he had ever battled seem to glisten back at him and he looked down again quickly, concentrating on fraying the fluorescent nylon.

"We gotta get you back in the water," he said, trying to keep the wobble from slinking between the gruff shelves of his voice. "I ain't having no curse upon me or be dragged to drowning by no sea witch."

"Sea witch!" The mermaid barked again. Mark stood up and stepped across the deck to the standing shelter. He started rummaging around in the various boxes and crates stacked in there. Freed from the Mark-barrier, Ray lurched in, throwing himself at the mermaid's tail.

"Surely you remember me Morveren, how we made sweet love by the light of the new moon, those salty kisses—"

The mermaid turned to him. "Did we, sweetie? And how did that work? Did you find the secret gloryhole that has eluded men for millennia, or did you just rub your floppy chubber against my tail until you came?"

Mark returned with his hands cupped together. Standing over the mermaid, he pulled them apart, releasing a showering of coins and trinkets. Ray jumped back.

"Hey!" She lifted her arms to shelter her head. "What the fuck are you doing?"

"I want you to leave; receive my offering of gold and treasure to appease thee." Mark stood there, trembling.

The mermaid plucked up a 2p as brown as mud.

Mark mumbled. "I know it ain't much, but that watch is worth a bit."

"Listen old man," the mermaid grabbed Mark's trouser legs, pulling down so hard he had to kneel before her to stop his overalls sliding down. She moved her hands one over the other, up his shirt, until she closed a fist around his beard, yanking that yellow-stained letterbox where his lips poked through down close to her face. Through the corner of his eye Mark could see the thick, chalky ridges of her nails and tried to hold his breath.

"I'm not letting you put me back," she said into his face. "You think this was an accident? I have a message for all you *filthy landshrimp*—" Mark whimpered as she pushed her vacuous eyes up close to his "—and you're gonna help me spread it to the world."

Ray stared open-mouthed at their closeness. "You know it's bad luck to have a time-piece on board," he muttered, snatching the watch off the mermaid's lap.

At around nine, last night's partygoers dragged their hangovers and wrecked bodies to the seashore to burn. Caught in their midst was

Ray's wife Nina, uncharacteristically late to the scene.

"Ray!" She bellowed, hauling her mass through the crowd, spindly bikini-ed teenagers ricocheting off her as she went. Her husband was like a magpie, flitting off to each new, shiny thing that winked in the sun.

"Ray, I know you're up there, and I'll be right up there with you in a minute." Nina couldn't keep her mouth and her eyes open at the same time, so that her eyes stayed closed the whole time she spoke, and only fluttered open at the last syllable —which was lucky for Ray because he didn't think he could take both her words and her looks at once.

Up on the deck, Ray flinched his hands back from the mermaid. As if drawn by some great magnet, he backed away and slid off the boat to join his vast wife.

"What's going on up there?" Nina asked him with her eyes firmly shut, pressing her bosom into him. Before he could answer, Chloe Wellington squeezed in past Nina and thrust her microphone paw into Ray's face.

"Mr. Thompson, I hear you've had exclusive interactions with the creature up on that boat, can ya tell us what you saw?"

Ray knew he would regret it later. But he also knew the boys from the King's Arms would be watching. He had to prove his old tales right once and for all.

He grabbed the microphone, stared his love-struck eyes into the camera and said, as clearly as his saggy, aged lips could make out: "Up there is my long-lost love, Morveren. My beautiful mermaid."

Chloe pushed the mic further. "You mean, you've had relations with this th—woman? Morveren, you say? Can you confirm for anxious viewers back home that the mermaid *is in fact* Cornish?"

Nina fumed in the background of the camera shot, before turning and rippling away into the crowd. It's hard being dull when a magpie only wants treasure.

The sun bobbed ever higher, fast weaving a day of such mad brilliance that to view it unfolding over blue sea and fine sand proved too much for some, and they covered their eyes. Chloe watched the interview replays, back hunched in her moist suit, but even that fish-fucker wasn't enough to knock people off the major news sites and into her ratings box. She needed the thing itself.

Returning to Piran, she ordered the drone over the boat. She felt like a military leader, wide-stanced behind the monitor as the wheeling digital bird began collecting footage of the curious woman hunched up on deck.

"Closer," she murmured, but then the shot was blocked, the fisherman standing guard.

She grabbed the headset off Piran's face with a rubbery twang to his cheek.

"Mr Towen?" she said.

Through the screen, she saw the fisherman look around for the disembodied voice. Behind him, the drone caught snatches of the strange woman, steely and dark.

Chloe pressed on, frantically directing Piran's driving with flaps of her hand. "Mr Towen, you've been a local fisherman all your life; can you comment on the depletion of fish stocks by unregistered merpeople?"

The fisherman locked eyes on the shifting drone and began to wail. Launching forward, he threw his arms about, sending the drone spinning off the boat to bob over the ducking crowd. Someone shouted: "Can't you read the signs?" and the lifeguards made their way towards Chloe and the weary Piran, their guardianship of life apparently including against the perils of cheap drones from news channels.

So, Chloe just interviewed everyone else instead. Ellie Clayton doing Hair and Beauty up at the college brandished her brushes between each finger, educating the masses about how to achieve the perfect mermaid-eye. A gaggle of pre-teens hastily concocted 'The Mermaid', whose sure-to-be viral status would release a much-craved serotonin shot into their addled, developing brains. Jack pulled off his shirt for the camera, fine sand glittering along his abs as he described how he was first on the scene, whilst doughy Henry glowered from high up in the lifeguard tower. Souvenir sellers appeared from nowhere, turning in from the brightest spots of sunlight with arms laden with every incarnation of mermaid merch, and Spence held up the crumpled photo of his daughter Yvey, whipped out by a riptide last July. Jean smoked in the background.

Chief Cuntstable Prynn gathered his men together like a rugby scrum, flipping his arms over their backs to make the huddle look more secret. PC Morgan shrugged it off.

"Stop fannying about Ian!" he said. "We've gotta take control of the situation here." The others bobbed their heads in agreement. "We can't have every Tom, Dick, and Harry turning up on our shores, claiming 'mermaid-status' and coming in unscrutinised. What message will that send? If you wanna sneak into Britain, Cornwall's the place to go."

"How do we know she's not from here?" piped up PC Putt. The youngest in the force, he had been to uni upcountry and thought he was better than the rest of them, according to mutterings in the King's.

"Have you looked at her?" Morgan spluttered. The head-bobbing paused. Morgan rushed on. "At the end of the day, she's an unidentified person, and it's our job to arrest unidentified persons and take them down to the anti-terrorism unit." The bobbing resumed.

PC Truscott stuck up his finger and rightly pointed out that: "We don't have a terrorism unit down here," and the others bobbed along.

"Enough!" Ian squealed, flapping his hands to shoo away the gaggle of heads. He straightened up and pulled his megaphone to his lips.

"Attention, ma'am. You are under arrest on suspicion of being here on illegal grounds. Please turn yourself in for police custody immediately."

The crowd started gabbling amongst themselves, releasing an equal number of cheers and boos. Students from the university combined bodyboards and markers for anti-deportation placards, and holidaying students recorded it all on their phones.

But there was no movement up on deck, just the face of Mark Towen occasionally popping up and peering down.

Mark was really starting to fret. A gathering group of fishermen stood at the edge of the crowd. Mark strained to hear through the wood, but only a few raised phrases drifted out from the general gravel of voices.

"Depletin' our fish stocks..."

"Stealin' our jobs..."

"Impossible quotas..."

Mark crammed his nails-fingers-knuckles-fist into his mouth. This was the last thing he needed. The harbours had been transformed into political arenas since the vote, and so far Mark had managed to stay well and truly out of it. The ocean was his whole life; he didn't want anything upsetting that. These young'uns with their chests up like anemones talking about 'taking back control of our waters'—Mark knew no one could control the sea. He looked over at the mermaid. He had to get her put back before she got strung up on a hook like some wayward shark.

"No one down there will listen to a word I say," he said, with a watery grin. "Got about as much clout down here as I do out there." He thumbed behind him at the blue expanse.

The mermaid was poking through the crates of gear stacked around her. "You've already done your bit. But you are more of a mouthpiece than you realise."

Mark looked back at the fishermen on the beach. He didn't want to know. He didn't want to be a mouthpiece. Why couldn't he just be a man who fished on his boat on the sea? "A mouthpiece for what?"

"I mean, you guys really were the emotional posterboys for the whole narrative." She turned back round, resting against the side. A long hook turned between her greyish fingers. Her tail twisted absentmindedly, never still. "The plucky little country making its way on its own. Small boats leaving rural harbours at dawn, braving all weathers to haul in an honest catch; using their generational knowledge of the sea to feed the nation. Powerful stuff really." She started to swing the hook round in small circles like a propeller.

Mark made a whine like a wet dog. "I'm telling you; you got the wrong guy."

"Plus, there's no way I would have survived coming up on one of the big guys. Too many I've known lost that way. You were—" She looked up at him through the rotating blade of the hook. "You *are* the perfect vessel."

"And what do you think'll happen to that vessel next time we go out? If I've taken a mermaid out of the sea? There'll be a swell and a lightning bolt with my name carved on it. You gotta go back!" He took a breath and then said again, quietly. "You have to let me put you back. There's no telling what any of *them* will do to you." He looked away. "There's no respect for the sea anymore."

The mermaid let her swirling eyes slip from his and focus back on the hook. "I'm not going back until I've said what I've come to say. I'm putting a stop to this."

Mark shook his head slightly, eyebrows knitted.

"To what?"

She sighed and a wave of bioluminescence shimmered along her length. "You up here arguing over quotas and percentages—carving up what does not belong to you. The fate of millions decided in some dried-up, desiccated landshrimp courtroom." She let go of the hook and it flew along the width of the boat, lodging into a plastic crate with a crunch. "I'm here to set it straight. From the sea-horse's mouth."

Mark groaned. In those dark eyes he saw it all: the lost ships, the empty nets. "Listen, love. The people down on that beach, they're not going to listen to you." He went to crouch next to her, but she fixed her eyes behind him and started flopping over the deck like a seal, all rolls of flesh and grunts and surprisingly fast as she made her way to the other side of the boat: the beach side. The side of freedom. Before she could throw her arm up over the side in greeting, he rugby tackled her down again.

"Just wait a minute, woman!"

Chief Cuntstable Prynn was gearing himself up for another announcement, nodding irritably to the furiously whispered corrections of PC Morgan, when a man in a blue waterproof outfit emerged from the body of the crowd, flanked by four or five other blue figures.

"Not so fast, PC Plod," the new voice boomed. "Whatever's up on that boat is out of your jurisdiction."

Ian Prynn looked up from beneath his red eyelids, swollen from the heat of the day and the heat of the situation and the heat of his uniform. "Who are you?"

The man was tall and strong, with tousled hair and a mouth wide enough for a lobster pot. He fixed his clear seaglass eyes on the blobby bobby. "We are the British Divers Marine Life Rescue, and we are here to protect that poor, sullied marine creature dragged up by human scum and return her to her rightful home," he snapped his head to look out over the rolling surf, "the big blue."

Listening up on the boat, hidden below the lip of the side, the mermaid spat. "Poor, sullied creature."

Mark bit his filthy nails. From behind, he noticed with a skin-crawling sensation that her entire grey back was in fact a writhing mess of tiny marine creatures. Like if you upturned a rock from a shallow pool.

"Stop right there," said another voice down on the beach. A tall, brunette girl with a horse-drawn face and jodhpurs appeared, clutching a small net and a clipboard. Behind her, more clipboards appeared with tall people attached, all wearing the freshly-scrubbed faces of the righteous. "We are the RSPCA, and we have reason to believe that that up there is an endangered species. It is our duty to transport the animal to a proper facility where it can be medically examined and properly protected."

The mermaid emitted two high-pitched clicks. "Keep your hands off me, coloniser." Mark was starting to wonder whether she was indeed the sacred daughter of the sea he had assumed her to be. He couldn't understand why she wanted to come onto land when all he wanted was to live out at sea. But maybe she would be okay.

Maybe he would be okay.

The mermaid suddenly pulled him down next to her. She pressed a finger to her lips.

"But I didn't say anythin—"

"Listen!"

Mark tuned in to the hubbub of voices from the beach.

"What?"

"That's it," the mermaid whispered. "That's the one!"

Mark had no idea what she was talking about, but as he listened, he started to pick out the smooth, controlled undulations of scripted speech from amongst the general hubbub.

"...And this is what it comes down to. This amazing *British* find beautifully demonstrates the richness of our nation's seas, and how we must work, tirelessly, as one, to protect our right to access such riches in the future."

Mark stuck his head up and looked down to see Chloe standing off to the left, interviewing a man with hair so dull it was almost colourless. A few strands hung down over his forehead, and he had small, wet, pink lips. He wore a dark blue suit and brown brogues, even in the twisting August heat. Even on a beach. Mark didn't know who, but he knew what he was.

The man continued, his animated, flabby face rolling up and over in time with his over-stressed intonations. "This is what's at stake unless we regain sovereignty of our seas. It begs the question: What if this incredible creature had been caught by a French or Portuguese shipping vessel?"

Chloe was nodding mechanically, one hand tucked into her armpit and the other holding the enormous microphone limply, looking like this was not the question she had begged. "Yes, all very fascinating Mr James, but I think what our viewers would like to know is, what is the government's official position on mermaids? Are they fish or are they people?"

Mark looked back down at the mermaid. "Him?"

The mermaid nodded. "That's who I need to speak to."

Mark looked at the grey, rubbery skin and the bulletproof tits and he decided he understood as little about this mermaid as he did any human on land. Was she even a *proper* mermaid? Would there even be a curse? Those foreboding swirls in her eyes now seemed to glimmer with hope rather than malice, like the round eyes of his grandchildren beside an ice cream van. He turned to the beach and waved at Chloe, who smushed a finger against the still-moving lips of the besuited man.

"She wants to speak to you," Mark jabbed at the politician. Even if there were repercussions for mer-napping, perhaps he could shift them onto somebody more deserving.

Chloe dipped forward into the shadow of Belle's hull, pressing an earpiece hard into the ossicles of her right ear. There had been a fair amount of commotion following Mark's invitation aboard, in which Chloe had slapped the Mr James several times across the face, telling him to get a hold of himself. The truth was that the North Cornwall MP, beyond some expected nerves, had a fairly good hold on himself and had resented the slapping. He had shaken Chloe off, turned and smoothed out his tie, before striding off to the ladder at the back of the boat. Chloe had stood watching him, twisting her hands together. She had been interviewing people all day, but she had yet to hear straight from the mermaid's mouth. Then, an idea had popped into her head, like an air bubble inside a clam, round with pearly promise. Lurching after James, she had grabbed his shoulder and whipped him round. She had pulled loose and then reknotted his tie, babbling about looking his best for the greatest meeting of his political career. The politician agreed and let her pull and straighten and smooth before turning and stepping toward the boat once more.

Beneath the hull, Chloe calibrated the receiver of the microphone. This was to be the most daring piece of investigative journalism ever conducted this side of the Tamar. That perv Simon Porter wouldn't know what hit him.

The politician's face was red, shiny, and grinning as he pulled himself up onto the boat.

"Sir," he grabbed Mark's hand and pumped it up and down. "Ryan James, your representative in government, as I'm sure you're well aware." Mark said nothing. Behind him, the mermaid smiled, twisting her tail around her in a traditional position.

The MP took in her unusual appearance, then chuffed like a small train and knelt in front of her.

"My lady!" said Ryan James, sweeping down into a low bow. Up close, her tail was pockmarked with scars and flaking delicately in the sun. He closed his eyes briefly, before opening them directly into her face. "It is just such an honour to meet you; our local, home-grown mermaid."

The mermaid nodded. "That's what I was hoping to talk to you about. I—"

"Excellent! I really cannot wait to hear all about your life down here in these, our British waters, and er, your excellent treatment at the hands of the inspirational Mr, er—" He looked up at Mark, who remained silent. "Well, this fine fishergentleman. Or should I say, the *nation*, cannot wait to hear, Morveren."

The mermaid tensed. "That is not my name. That's just what that disgusting landshrimp has been calling me." She jerked her head in the direction of the beach and the still-raving Ray. "I've never seen him before in my life. He doesn't speak for me." She stuck out her chin. "He's got nothing to do why I'm here." She drew herself up straight like a cobra. "The commercial fishing in this area—"

"Right, yes, of course—however, I don't think we should be so quick to hang Morveren out to dry, you know?"

Mark winced.

"It has this ring of authenticity; echoes the local area and the language. I think it can do great things for our image. Your image."

The mermaid raised her eyebrows. "I'll only go on record using my real name."

The MP swelled, gaseous with all the initial thoughts he had supressed for these past thirty years in public office. "Naturally, although we must consider the inevitable pronunciation difficulties. Where is that, er, remarkable accent from if you don't mind me asking—?"

The mermaid tipped her head back, opened her gullet, and emitted a series of squeaks and high-pitched wails. It sounded like a dolphin mixed with the wind moving through a crevice. Below the boat, Chloe wondered how she was going to transcribe such a sound.

The MP laughed, his head bobbing away from the mermaid as he stood, pulling the rest of his body with him. "Of course, whatever you need." Then he turned to Mark with a rubbery grin. "Must've had your hands full with this catch today, eh mate!"

The mermaid raised up on her tail. "Excuse me—"

"I ain't your mate," said Mark. He wasn't one to rock the boat (what kind of fisherman would he be if he did?) but nothing made him clam up like a politician. They mixed with the sea about as well as an oil spill.

The mermaid began again. "Mr James, I would appreciate it if we could use this time to discuss the matter at hand. The marine life in these waters is being massacred to a degree that simply cannot continue—"

The MP fixed Mark with a frown-smile like every corner of his face was being crushed inward. "There might have been a problem with overfishing in the 90s, but that's long since stabilised. Isn't that right, sir?" Mark gazed longingly out to sea.

"Stabilised!" The mermaid gave a hoot. "How can you describe the murder of millions of beings as 'stable'? What about that to you is—"

"Ah, I see. Didn't realise we had a cod hugger on our hands." James chuffed, the plastic smile never slipping from his face.

Below the hull, Chloe's eyes and mouth were both open as she listened to the tinny voices coming through her receiver. Piran approached her with something about returning to the studio and she kicked him in the shin. He hobbled away, muttering about how this was obviously misaligned resentment for Simon Porter.

James continued. "Miss, you can't know the complexities involved in managing national fisheries; an extremely difficult task but *with British control*—"

"It doesn't matter if it's the British or the French or the fucking Chinese," said the mermaid. "I am here to tell you that this genocide—" Here, James let out a hoot of his own, "—must end."

"Okay. So, would you propose... what? Stop fishing completely?"

"Commercial, industrialised fishing, yes."

"Miss, forgive me, but what an incredibly naive thing to say. Frankly, it's clear you have, at best, a very basic understanding about how the world works—"

"I've got an excellent understanding—it's my world you're eating."

The MP exhaled. Mark was leaning against the side of the boat, smoking. He had watched this all unfold, the weight of responsibility gently lifting off him like mist from the dawn waves. She might have tits of a kind, but that weren't no mermaid. That was just a crazy talking fish.

The MP straightened his suit, backing away. "Thank you for your time, Morveren." The mermaid bristled. "I'll be sure to raise your concerns with the appropriate department, this er," he made his fingers into twin bunnies of mockery, "this 'genocide' of fish." He let off a little steam. The mermaid's breathing was now ragged. "Best of luck to you!"

He walked off down the deck, raising his hand in a gun shape up above him, like he was starting a race. "And remember, be sure to vote Ryan James next February!"

The mermaid drooped, as she and Mark watched as the ticket out of their respective messes disappeared down the ladder. But just as his forgettable, colourless head disappeared, a strand of blonde hair snaked into view.

"I wonder if I may be able to help," purred Chloe.

As the sun dropped down from its whining pinnacle into a warm, orange balm with a sigh, pleasantly exhausted from the weight of its own brilliance, the crowd around the boat slowly but completely forgot all about the mermaid up on the deck. The RSPCA and the British Divers Marine Life Rescue knelt in a small circle comparing legislation and paperwork, and the policemen whined around them like gnats. The students repurposed their placards into windbreaks and caught rays, and the children were herded up by mothers and grandmothers and occasionally fathers, who wiped heat-and-sand-induced tears away with soothing lines like, "The mermaid has to go back into the sea now, she has to have her dinner too, she's very tired and has to go to bed as well, just like you my love," and the kids sniffed and clutched one shell in their sand-raw fingers and whispered, like it was the saddest and most true thing they'd ever said, "What do mermaids eat?" and the mothers and grandmothers and the occasional father were already up and looking for their beach camp with frowns and burnt faces and saying, "Oh you know, seaweed and crabs and fish and waves," and the kids frowned because that didn't seem right but before they could question their guardians further they were being thrust a packet of crisps or a ham sandwich or maybe some carrot sticks, which they pushed into their faces and forgot about everything else. Jean and Spence went home with their grief and Ray Thompson drifted back to the pub with the other men to speak of the great lost love of his youth, which was better in the soft butter-glow of memory than with strange greyish skin scornfully rejecting him in the present. Mark Towen, feeling the boat hitch up into weightlessness once more, moved past the crumple of empty nets and started the engine, backing out into the shallows.

Slumped on the floor outside the bathroom in overcrowded carriage C of the Great Western Railway, Chloe Wellington gave an exhausted little grin. The Good Morning Britain segment was confirmed; it was really happening. She tried not to think about the 'afters'; the questions; the humiliation; the butchering. The ticket officer came by and she hand him her inordinately expensive slip of card.

"How long they been in there?" the man said, nodding to the closed toilet door.

Chloe's hand shot up to the handle. "Oh, that's just my daughter. Four. She insists on going by herself like a big girl!"

The officer blinked, his years in customer service having sanded away all notion of children's charm.

Chloe smiled wider. "Her ticket should be included in mine?"

He looked at her slip again. "Oh yes. Sorry." He handed it back to her and wobbled off down the carriage.

Scrunched up on the other side of the door, the mermaid snoozed peacefully, her tail flushing water on itself each time the tank refilled.

In her dreams, she was singing, stringing up rows and rows of landshrimp.

Landshrimp presenters, landshrimp technical support and landshrimp audience; their eyes glassy, their guts removed.

HOT AND BOTHERED

"You can't hog them all!" Chloe leaned forward from the backseat of the car. "Give them here!"

She made a strained snatch with her sweaty little palm, but Daniel, in the front seat, moved the Cheestrings further out of his sister's reach. He gave a snort and Chloe floundered with her arm. "Give iiiiiiiit!"

"Kids, stop it." Holly gripped the steering wheel with tired, tense claws. She was too old for this. It was Saturday, it was the middle of the summer holidays and the roads leading out from Asda were clogged with beachward traffic. She wasn't going to the beach; she was doing jobs for grandma.

Holly gazed blankly into the shimmering back window of the car in front of her. She noted the silhouettes of three small heads sitting quietly in the backseat. The sunroof gave way to a folded, vintage parasol sticking up into the blue, and through the open driver's seat window, a slim, perfectly tanned, seemingly wrinkle-free elbow appeared, a tasteful flower tattoo swirling up the forearm. The hand was waving a pair of sunglasses lazily in the sunlight, reflecting it directly into Holly's eyes. That mum may be stuck in traffic now, Holly thought, but she was about twenty minutes away from releasing her lovely, quiet kids into the freezing surf and enjoying a nice glass of white wine. It would probably be the perfect temperature due to some miracle cool bag. She'd just have the one before resuming her role as bat and ball champion and sandcastle queen, rather than sinking into a vat of the stuff like a crocodile into a swamp. Behind her, Holly felt her youngest, Millie, kicking her seat. She winced: right in her slipped disc.

"Mum!"

"What?"

"Daniel is not sharing!" Chloe's spit misted her ear. Holly set her teeth and didn't answer, pretending to listen to the *Sizzling Summer Hits* blasting from the CD player. She heard snuffling next to her and turned to look at Daniel. Moist tentacles of florescent orange cheese writhed from his mouth. He looked like some horrifying alien beast. His hands were busily ripping apart the lithe, plastic bodies of more Cheestrings, before jamming his fingers into the sides of the overflowing cavity. "Mum, he's gonna eat them allll," persisted Chloe, jumping between the two front seats and shaking her body like a banshee.

"Daniel, will you please share the Cheestrings with your sister," said Holly, releasing the clutch to inch forward a few metres before stopping again and pulling on the handbrake. She leant her arm on the open windowsill, pulling her hair away from the back of her neck. She fanned her chest. The chorus on the song had finished and now the rap break had come in. Millie rapped along with startling accuracy. "Millie, language," Holly snapped behind her.

"Sorry," Millie called in a sickly-sweet voice before diving right back in, delivering another swift kick to her mother's spine. Holly jolted forward. She picked her top away from her damp skin; she could feel the heat building. Not *now*, she thought.

"Mum, he's eaten all of them!" Chloe shouted. Daniel cackled.

"Daniel!" Holly snapped. "Chloe, there's Dairyleas in the boot."

The song ended yet the same song seemed to come on again, but even louder. Holly exhaled and flapped at her chest with both hands, but there was no air. The lights up ahead turned green

44

and the car in front pulled off to the right, following the packed road to the beach. Holly got a brief glimpse of her more fortunate double; effortless up-do, open-mouthed laugh. Their car swung away, and Holly pressed up into second gear, inching along to the bungalow estate where grandma lived. Her shopping would be roasting in the boot. Her milk would be warm. Her bread would be sweaty. She would moan. Holly wiped beads from her forehead, trying to control the furnace moving through her. The line of traffic halted again.

From the back came a blood-curdling scream. "What the hell is it now?" Holly yelled, wrenching her head round. She felt her neck unspool, her spine rippling in a horsewhip of pain and she cried out. Chloe was kneading Millie with bare legs, pushing down her tiny dark head as she dived headfirst into the boot. "Chloe, get off Millie now!" Holly's voice cracked. Daniel turned up the music. A car beeped from behind and Holly faced forward, teeth gritted, and pushed down the handbrake, moving into first to trundle along the beating heat of the clogged road. Pain seared through her neck and she felt a burning screech building in her belly.

Chloe sang tunelessly as she rooted around in the boot, oblivious that her pants were showing beneath her hiked sundress. Between sobs, Millie reached up with tiny, pale fingers and pulled them down to her ankles, exposing Chloe's bottom to the baking car interior. Chloe roared and fell on Millie, slapping and spitting and swearing. Daniel thrust himself back and forward in time with the pounding music in the front and Holly began to scream at her kids, screaming at them to please stop fighting and why couldn't they be nice to each other for one second and how she was stressed, so stressed she might die and now they were late and would you just let me finish and now grandma would be pissed and oh great, *now* I'm having a hot flush and she started to cry and there was no air and a moan began to rise, clinging roundly to the sobs bubbling wetly up her throat.

The car jolted to a halt and Holly began to inhale in huge gasps, but no oxygen was coming in and the heat was unbearable, an all-consuming heat that stretched through her like a hand inside a puppet. The kids were still arguing and pointing at one another, Chloe's face a twisted mess of hate and Millie crying and apologising in the back, trying to stroke Holly's hair but her sticky palms dragged on the strands and ended up pulling it. Holly tried to focus on something beyond the flush rising through her, but she could feel herself slipping even as she gripped the steering wheel, her knuckles blooming white.

Suddenly, the wheel began to buckle and warp in her hands. A roar was building deep inside her, drowning out the shitty pop tune and the traffic and the squabbling monsters all around her in the car as she began to swell. The roar was one of terrible, primeval depth, like the mournful call of a leviathan wounded in some great battle. It rattled up inside the cavernous walls of Holly, walls that had conceived, carried and contracted to spit out these three smaller beasts; beasts that now shrank back in horror as their mother grew like a triffid in the front seat, their cries silenced. Daniel turned off the CD player.

Holly's skin split and she got so big she pushed through the car roof with a metal-twisting screech and the children began shrieking themselves, scrabbling against the car doors. The roar that had been slowly building, rattling up the well of Holly's being like an escaped poltergeist, ripped through her mouth now as she shot up to be twenty, fifty, a hundred feet tall, with bulging tentacles splitting out of her and writhing around like swollen Cheestring tendrils, thrashing down on vehicles all around her to the splintering sound of glass.

She panted; finally, some air. She looked down and spotted her children cowering together in the road, their scrawny arms cut with glass, and terror in their piggy little eyes. "How could I have spawned such monsters?" she bellowed down at them. In that moment, she saw them for what they were: parts of herself she'd expelled. She could feel herself metamorphosing still, the outline of a veiny batwing cutting across her peripheral vision and something pushing up through her temple. Smoke began to puff through her nostrils as she threw around her monstrous head. It felt good to blow off some steam.

The street was in total chaos as cars piled up and fires broke out. People streamed from their vehicles in wiggling ant lines. She picked up a nearby car with one gigantic claw and crushed its middle. Turning it on its side, she shook out a hysterical woman through the driver's seat window into her other claw.

"I slave," she yelled down at her children as she threw the woman into an adjacent field, "and I slave," she tipped out a tiny boy and flung him away too, "and I slave." She gripped the car in both hands and shook out a man and a dog and a whole load of other crap out onto the road below, before hurling the wreckage after the mother and son into the field. "And for what?" Her children looked up at her in horror. "Not even a thank you." Holly turned and trampled over the cars down the street: "No appreciation, no 'how are you feeling today, Mum?', not even a cursory thought about anything *I* might be going through!" She drove her arms through office blocks and apartment buildings; rubble cascaded down onto the alarm-filled street below. She noticed the 'To the Beach!' road sign winking in the sunlight and she plucked it out from the concrete like a toothpick. "Do I get to go and relax at the beach today?" She wrapped her scaly hands around a group of fleeing beachgoers. "No, I have to go and see my ungrateful mother, and listen to her bitch and moan about me getting the wrong type of fruit scones." She skewered one of the tourists on the pointed end of the sign. "Listen to her go on and on about what a perfect brother I have," she slid another teen onto the pole, "when he does absolutely—" she went to pierce the belly of the third youth, when the sun lotion coating his body caused him to slip through her fingers and drop to the pavement below, "—oh fuck," said Holly. She turned and threw the whole endeavour in the direction of the sea.

She stood for a minute, gazing out to the glittering, azure horizon, before turning and stomping forlornly back down the street. The flush was passing; she was starting to cool down. She dropped down next to the KFC, hooked her claws over the roof and began peeling it back like a sardine can. "I'm not asking for a lot; I just want you kids to get along. Just be nice to each other, so I can have a little bit of peace." She started picking up wailing customers and popping them into her mouth. She was guilt-eating. Everyone at Slimming World had highlighted it as her big trouble-area. Eventually, she let her claw drop down, and she sighed, looking out at the smoke-filled street strewn with bodies and carnage. "Shit."

She uprooted a nearby tree and began to fan herself. The flaming tendrils of heat that had gripped her not ten minutes ago had basically receded, gobbled back into the dark hole at her centre. A big, gaping maw where babies used to grow. It had felt sad when it had first opened up, but on days like this Holly wondered if there was a way she could push her current ones back in there—swallow them up into nothingness. She satisfied the craving with fast-food customers instead.

From the direction of the beach, she began to hear faint crashes. Probably the navy showing up to restrain me, Holly thought mauvely. But through the narrow streets, picking her way through the torn metal and petrol fires, appeared another, enormous beast. She had scorpion's pincers and sprawling legs ending in cloven hooves, a tarantula's abdomen bristling with hairs and a mess of snake heads.

Holly watched as the woman slung her twenty or so heads around in each direction, gripping the edges of two adjacent buildings with her pincers. She seemed nervous. Holly gave her a wave of her tentacles and the monster hurried over, trampling several still-fleeing pedestrians as she went. She sank down next to Holly.

"Oh my god, am I glad to see you," she laughed.

Holly smiled in response, continuing to chew slowly. She felt rude and reached out the half-eaten carcass of a KFC patron. "Legs?"

The woman exhaled. "I couldn't eat. You don't have a cigarette, do you?"

Holly swallowed. "Sorry." The woman shrugged and they both surveyed the scene. Holly coughed into a tentacle and blushed. "I, er—I think I got a little carried away this time."

The woman shook her many heads. "This is not that bad. You should see the mess I made down the beach—like a bomb's gone off down there!"

Holly laughed.

"I'm Chloe, by the way," said the scorpion woman.

Holly grimaced. "Oh god, that's my daughter's name." She buried her face in her tentacles. "I screamed at them so much. It's not even their fault really, I just cannot cope with them at the minute."

Chloe's reptilian heads nodded in unison. "I had to bind and gag mine earlier under the guise of some 'kidnapped by pirates' game just to get a moment's peace."

"Right? They're still so young. And such hard work. Everything is difficult and I just don't have the energy anymore." Holly stopped and looked at Chloe, who raised her eyebrows but didn't say anything. She went on. "Especially with this on top of everything else." Holly gestured vaguely to the scene around her and her own mutated body. She had felt shy about talking about it in the past, like she was admitting she wasn't strong enough. But the presence of Chloe's bristling abdomen next to her own ever-squirming tentacles comforted her, and she felt the weight of their monstrosity shared between them. "I don't even feel like myself half the time."

"We're changing into something else," Chloe agreed. "But maybe that's a good thing."

Holly shrugged. "I guess. I certainly don't need any more." She looked up towards where her car must have been. "I hope they're alright."

"D'you know what? Screw them," said Chloe, raising herself up onto her eight legs. "Let's take some time off. Some proper time off for once. For ourselves."

Holly slithered upright. "Yeah?"

"Definitely. The army will be here any minute so we should probably head off anyway." Chloe looked up into the blue. "It's such a nice day."

Holly grinned. "Go on then."

"I ripped the awnings off a few bars down the beach—I bet they'll float," said Chloe. She offered one huge pincer. A tasteful flower tattoo swirled up its forearm. "Although I don't know where we're going to get a drink big enough."

Holly linked up her own bulging tentacle. "I'm sure there'll be some kegs knocking around."

"Shots!" said Chloe, and they strolled on down the blood-streaked road to the glittering azure of the sea.

THE ROOT CAUSE

"Scalpel."

Greta places the knife into my hand. I make a neat line down the donor's chest, unzipping her torso. Her breasts peek out from beneath the mint-green sheet like deflated balloons; nipples dark and sad. The sheet covers her face.

"Clamp."

My hand waits, empty.

Greta is peering out from our illuminated circle into the darkness of the theatre. She is looking for the man who clapped his hand over our mouths at two in the morning, dragged us from our beds. Who'd herded us through the caterwauling streets here to MyCel ("it's pronounced my-seal"). Greta explosive with questions, me trying to place his smell. Citrus.

And now he's in here somewhere. Occasionally, we hear a drawer open, the clink of root vials on the shelf, but we need to focus.

"Where's Bea?" Greta whispers, barely.

"Clamp."

Above Greta's mask, the skin around her eyes folds down. Worry wings, I called them when she was just a kid. Too cute now.

She lifts the clamp from the surgical tray, dislodging another tool and it clatters, metal on metal. In the corner, something moves.

Greta whips round. "You should be wearing a mask, you know," she says, her voice a trapped bird in the air-pressured space.

"Greta, shut up."

I pin back rolls of muscle, exposing the hard line of the sternum. Greta's been with me since I found her running around the alleys with a leash around her neck, yet more old country spawn mopped up by the new corps. I took her back to the caves, one of our last strongholds. Trained her up, gave her the skills – but you can't take the street-fight out of someone like that. She won't last long in MyCel, with its mint-green walls and sterilised instruments. The glass doors that close with a beautiful suction sound, like a fridge.

On our first day here, we couldn't stop playing with them; me inside, Greta out. Slumpf. I'd watched her face through the frost-tinged glass, laughing soundlessly. Our own practice. The three of us.

Not quite my name outside, but on the high street and a licence to operate.

Two of us, usually. Bea off chasing glitter.

"Saw."

Greta hands it to me and then fidgets with the cloth covering the donor's face. I slap her hand, eyes on the corner. Sharp and citrus. I've smelt it before.

"It's wrong." Greta's voice is too loud. "How can we take this from them when we don't even know their name?"

G-ma's eyes blazing. *Indiscriminate.*

I ignore her, switch on the oscillating saw and start to carve through the sternum. Blood and flakes of bone spit at me. All those years out the back of a girls' bar in cardboard city, up a flight of stairs populated by rats grown feisty from scavenging on brain, trying to process the memories they were eating. We never knew when a gang 'collector' would show up. But still. More hallowed than this. G-ma kicking the shrink-wrapped catalogues. *You're spitting on the ancient ways.*

I switch off the saw and push it into the open air where Bea usually stands. I almost drop it, my sleep-deprived brain running on autopilot. Where is she? Not in bed when Citrus Hands came along.

I let her face drain from my mind before I get distracted.

"Retractor."

Reaching out from the maniacal grin of the open chest, the donor's ribs are like huge, elongated teeth. Inside, the heart jumps around like a panicked gerbil. I watch its movement, trying to feel it in step with my own heartbeat, but I can only hear the clock. I need to hear its voice, but G-ma's pulses in my head. *This is not some plastic surgery, like those corps will teach you. It means something.*

I concentrate. It's faint, but I can hear it—just. Whinnying, but soft. "'Get out, get out,'" I whisper in the old language, letting it speak through me.

There's a shrill splinter of a dropped vial. I jump before I can stop myself. Greta gasps.

The day we were 'approached' by MyCel, the Liaison and his goons had just wandered into our cardboard city practice, him speaking of global markets and worker protection. The Liaison had been exquisite looking, his lips carved from coral. I was not expecting it but braced myself; Greta too. Bea's bottom lip limp. They'd hung around until an extraction, then watched silently as we worked on a ten-year-old girl. Afterwards, the Liaison had only said one thing.

I listen to the heart and reply. "I am a friend."

Less talking, more slicing, he'd said.

"Retractor!"

Greta swears and runs to Bea's side of the operating table. The donor whispers back 'retractor' in the old language.

They should be asleep. G-ma's practice, in the caves. *Writhing* anaesthetic makes the root seize up, and post-extraction it is dull; cracked. Harder to sell to a discerning client. Like how you can taste fear in meat if the animal dies writhing. She'd looked at me over the open body steaming in the night air. *Bad meat does not sell.*

It does these days. There are plenty of anaesthetised extractions by unrooted practitioners, but with MyCel, you get authenticity. The Liaison's lips had said. "You people know the history. It's in your bones."

The donors should be sleeping, dreaming about something pleasant and uncomplicated, with good colours. Back in cardboard city, we had to rely on old methods to control dream content, but now regulation and foreign money have brought in the drugs, with several infusions being trialled already. Judging from this donor's breathing, her buyer has managed to get her on such a batch. At significant additional cost.

I slide two fingers beneath the beating heart. It recoils from my touch like a slug to salt and, barely a whisper, I repeat, shakily: "I am a friend."

It relaxes.

I coax it upwards, sweating despite the air con. I try to let Bea and Citrus Hands and the Liaison and G-ma and all my doubts melt away—

Slumpf. I look up. A masked assistant from the adjoining theatre stands there, hands held up with fingers spread, blood clots webbing between their mint-green gloves. Whoever pulled this off thought of everything.

"Wipe," I croak, and Greta is back with me, dabbing my forehead. I pause and take a slow, rattling breath.

G-ma never used to have any water before an extraction, a whole day at least. *A bead of sweat onto an exposed heart poses great risk.* Her words raspy in the heat. *The heart is an uneasy creature, like our deer so often bound for open graves at roadside.* I feel this heart heaving against its constraints. One drop of sweat would be enough, my intention revealed – and all its nervousness would have fallen away. It would have swelled then stilled, sacrificing its host to bar my way to the root beneath.

This is the part that scuppers so many unrooted practitioners. Table deaths are high, but it doesn't deter the desperate. Even a nail-sized lump of root can fetch more than they would ever make in cardboard city. It used to be a gift given in sacrifice. Now it is sold to patch up the hollow-chested.

I whisper to the heart, words I don't even know the meaning of, soothing it until it is limp and pliable. Lifting it, I catch my breath.

It's even better than I imagined.

This is an exceptional root. Its branches are muscular, like a good sprig of ginger, and the colour moves through it like summer sun.

Mine and Greta's eyes meet. Who is this buyer? Prime dream sedative, midnight extraction. Another vial drops to the floor and I recognise the citrus smell. It's bleach.

Anyone with enough money can repair their own decaying root: bolster a crumbling trunk before the rot completely melts through, or create an ornate structure that blooms through their entire torso. It used to be a complex, spiritual exchange, but with MyCel there are catalogues with roots separated into categories, star ratings in different characteristics. 'Strong sense of community'. 'Affinity with nature'. 'Rituals for ancestors'. The Liaison, ten-year-old root held up to the light. "What does this root have that mine doesn't?"

This root wasn't in the catalogue.

The donor coughs and we freeze. I've got two fingers tucked beneath her heart and the smell of flesh is so strong I can chew it. I once had a woman sleepily rub her eyes and glance down to see her chest being sawed open and that was that. Dead before I could even scream "Retractor!" at Bea. I still raced inward, ripping the ribcage open with my bare hands and roughly pushing the heart aside, but it was no use. The root was as black and wrinkled as a burnt carrot.

But this woma–donor gurgles–then stills. I swallow, forgetting the smell–big mistake–and race on.

"Shears."

Greta already has them ready. I snip through the branches of the root that connect it to the donor's innermost being, and lift it out, letting the heart flop back down into the hollow cavity beneath it. I cradle the root in my bloodied gloves like a newly whelped pup, turning from the steaming crater. "There we are, here we go," I say to it, my voice shaky. "It's going to be okay."

Behind me, I hear the frenzied electrocardiogram as the heart feels the absence, and frantically casts round for its charge. I walk towards the glass doors to the adjoining theatre. There is a bloody handprint at shoulder height, black in the low light.

I think of G-ma in her cave, no adjoining theatre, just two bodies side by side. *This thing is sacred. And you are the link between them.*

"Kloe."

I turn back to Greta, who is bent over. She has pulled back the white sheet to reveal Bea's sleeping face. Her bottom lip is limp. A molecule of glitter winks on her eyelid.

Someone lets out a call like an animal. I stagger, almost dropping the root. The citrus hands appear from the darkness and he has a knife; not an extraction knife, a proper knife. I regain my footing, cradling the root closer.

"No," I manage to say. "It has to be me."

"Kloe!" Greta is sobbing as I place my hand over the handprint on the vacuumed glass door that sounds like a fridge. Slumpf. And walk through into the adjoining theatre. In here, there are no screams. The transplant must be done quickly, for the root will soon shrivel without a body to inhabit. Without Bea's body. Someone makes that moan again.

On the table, the Liaison is lying slumbering and cleaved. Some ashen porridge lies scraped against the side of the kidney dish beside him. The preparatory team swim away with my tears and I step into the spotlight to perform the transplant.

JULIE'S PLACE

Three rights. One out of the lift, the doors closing behind me in time, the next stepping through the sticky green door, then finally past number 12 looking straight ahead to 13, rounding the corridor to face my new flat.

("It must be really *amazing* to have your own space again," my mum laughed dry and hollow on the phone. "So much better than being cooped up down here." I could see her in the kitchen like a whirling dervish, an item from every room in the house in her multiplying arms. How did she do it?)

Around me, the walls were faded pink, with blue trim. ("An abandoned hotel," my Spanish roommate Eva had said in a faux-ghost voice as I loaded our stuff into the lift on move-in day. Me jamming the button again and again; her just standing there, picking her pimples. Not really my own space again.)

It was only 2 p.m. though, so Eva was not home from work yet. I went in and set them down on the counter; blood-tipped, deep maroon and Aloe-man, one two three. The succulents were already taking on personalities.

Houseplants came doctor recommended, and succulents are the hardest to kill. *Nice and easy*, said every blog ever.

I moved to the kitchen sink under the window and drew water down into a brandy glass, watching the sun rub its cheek along the pebbledash wall of the perpendicular tenements. I could pick up three a week for the whole year, very affordable. Then my flat would be bursting with succulents; nice and juicy. Haha. A fresh start. Back in the city.

I left the flat again at 5.15, cutting it a little fine but I didn't see Eva on my way out. There was a proliferation of good coffee shops nearby, many of which were open late. A couple streets over, CULT demanded a high level of puritanical discomfort with its bare brick and exposed piping. The barista didn't stop talking to the man leaning on the other end of the counter the whole way through taking my order. They must have been mates. As I waited to pay, the barista finally looked at me. He was quite good-looking really, maybe I'd get to know him over the weeks and he'd suddenly notice me after coming in and ordering the same thing hundreds of times and say, "Hey, you're the one that always has a double soy latte, extra foam—" and I'd nod shyly. Or maybe not, maybe I'd raise my eyebrows or stick out my chin, and he'd lean across and smile slowly and speak to me like he does that man down the other end—

"No more avocado, sorry." I snapped back, but he was talking to someone behind me. "She got the last of it," he said, jerking his head at me.

The person behind me let out a slow exhalation. "Seriously?"

Feeling ashamed, I glanced back. She had a thick, poorly cut fringe chopped an inch above her eyebrows and I knew she deserved that avo toast so much more than me.

"Sorry," I wheezed.

She looked at me with half-closed lids. "I'll just have to share yours." Her smile was slow, letting it build, then break, then crash over into a laugh like a wave. Such control.

I smiled back like a grandma who didn't get the joke, collected my tea and wandered over to a table in the back. A few minutes later, she plopped herself down opposite me.

Her fringe was home-cut because all hairdressers were in the employ of the government, and you know there's *someone* in Global South dying for their dyes. "Right?" she said.

"Right." I cleared my throat. I looked down at my food. Did she really want to share? "Anyway, it looks nice."

"Thanks." She blew upwards, ruffling a few of the strands and laughing throatily. She wasn't wearing any make-up, and she had a nose ring like a bull. I imagined a little beanie-d boyfriend, a mini, grow-your-own-in-water-overnight companion pulling on it during sex, knocking it slowly back and forth on her nostril whispering: *Let me in girlie.* She was so natural and how could glasses from a grandad look so cool. She managed it.

Her name was Julie and she was an artist (my mum's distraught face loomed in my mind). "Been working in the city for a couple years now. It's pretty cool, we have a studio down by the canal." Her voice had a low, gravel drawl from pulling on rollies during dirty raves since she was 14. I imagined. Her nails were painted chalk-blue.

"What kind of stuff do you do?" I burned my tongue on my green tea. I had wanted a coffee, but the apparatus they handed out for self-assembly had looked too complicated for smooth construction. Especially in front of *An Artist* (I felt my mum's finger pushing through a gap in my neurons: "Now is this wise pet, more artists? You know how... *involved* you can get—" but I strangled her with an axon. I axed her. Haha). Besides, coffee was imperialist now, apparently.

"I mainly do conceptual stuff." She pushed her hand up under her hair, close to her neck, piling it up on top of her head to stick out at a weird angle. Her eyes had green flecks in them.

Should I proffer my own art world dalliances here? Like a job interview?

Is it a dalliance if you lose your mind?

The shiny flecks in her eyes had dulled, drifting out the window to the ice-wet street. Not emerald, but seaglass maybe.

They flashed back on, as though she had just remembered we were having a conversation.

"I'm *completely* obsessed with this 90s artist. She was an American environmentalist with like, a totally radical agenda." Her pupils poked up towards me through the thick grey of her lids. "Paula Hernsheist." It wasn't a question; more a statement to confirm my obvious obliviousness.

I opened my mouth, but before I could pretend, she cut me off. "She's pretty underground. She did these amazing performances; you know The Broadcast? It's my favourite thing ever."

I shook my head.

"She was part of this commune, on the coast, made up of these really interesting like-minded people who were trying to get people to, just like, *listen* y'know?" She stopped again. Pulled out her phone.

"Listen to what?" I probed. "What did they broadcast?"

She looked up. "Oh yeah, so it was on like early morning, like 6 a.m. TV. Some kids programme—I can't remember which. Anyway, her and this bunch of other artists from her commune hijack the station and chloroform the puppeteers and put on the puppets. Then the characters start swapping these radical slogans yeah, like—" She pushed her chin down into a thin, barely a double, chin. "'The white man sucks dry his own dick of racist and sexist agendas!' and all stuff with nuclear disarmament and animal rights and stuff, and the parents dozing on the sofas behind the playpens don't even really register what's happening for ages 'cos it's still just the visuals of the puppets." She took a sip of her tea.

Her voice hadn't risen in volume at all, maintaining the same monotonous drawl. It matched her eyelids, though looking closer I could see tiny networks of blue and red being forged through the grey skin: noble explorers.

"This goes on a way until the kids start absorbing it, parroting the slogans over the breakfast table. That's how they got their message out, y'know."

I sipped my tea. What message?

Back at home, I wiped my eyeliner off in the mirror, blinking at the flat, axolotlian face blinking back in time with me. I didn't know how to feel about Julie. Whether I wanted to scorn her, kiss her, or kill her and wear her skin. Great. Just like any man on the planet. This is why we're fucked.

Eva hung about my room as I tried to get ready, rolling my rejected eyeliners across the desk with a puzzled look. I snatched them off her and put them in my bedside drawer. She flounced on to the bed.

"Who is she anyway?" she asked, picking a pimple on the inside of her thigh.

"No one. Someone I met at the coffee shop," I replied, looking around for my bag. I barely had enough time to be late.

Eva flopped onto her stomach. "Which coffee shop?"

I didn't say anything. She thumbed through the books on my bedside table. She was in here too much. Her skin was offensively tanned. I could never even see these 'pimples' she so obsessively picked.

"Who is *Herman Neutics*?"

I stared very hard at the 'pimple' on her leg."

Anyway. Come out with us tonight. We are having a roof party at Global. Emerald Gin is sponsoring; there will be DJs and the fire pit and ah! It will be *so much* fun. Oh, come!" She rolled around like a calf. She worked in marketing or for a hedge fund or a lawn bank or something ("Eva is just doing *amazing* things," Mum had cooed, finally off the phone. Her friend's daughter was moving house. Yes, in the city. Why of course she'd take me in. Take me under her wing, feed me regurgitated corporate success. She'd be happy to. "She'll be a great person to have around, lots of connections. You know, in life, there are radiators and drains, and Eva is just, she is just..." Mum had taken a rare pause in her interminable whirlwind to smile brightly as she watched me pack from the bedroom doorway. "She'll do you good. Keep you grounded." I'd stayed quiet).

"I'm okay, thanks," I said, grabbing the book from her. At the door, I scanned the mess of the room, checking I had everything.

"Come onnnnnnn," Eva called with her big, white smile. She bounced in front of me. "They always serve this *amazing* pulled pork burgers—you will love them."

I looked up at her bright, made-up face and felt a sneer sidling out me, awakened from its dormant state. "I'll skip the butchery if you don't mind," I said, before turning to leave.

I walked the mile to Julie's place. The wires holding spring to winter were spindling, snapping and pinging above my head. This time last year, I had just met her. Those last crucial few months before dissertation hand-in. That spring felt like someone had dug up a dead hand and was trying to warm it between their thighs. Everyone was at it. The pigeons had tripled in size, bloated males waddling after the females, cooing reassuringly ("C'mon baby, I'll make you feel goooo-gooood!") Seagulls roared at each other, whilst the tits whipped into tornadoes above the hedges. Or maybe I was projecting. Making excuses. It was nature; nature made me do it!

I felt swollen in the car next to her.

I shook my head, quickly closing down the memory before its overplayed conclusion.

Julie's place wasn't just by the canal; it extended over it on rusting steel supports.

"Dunno, summin to do with fishing probably," Julie responded when I asked her what the building used to be. It was early evening, and in the main sitting room were collected a small cluster of creatives, peering through the dusty ferns that climbed the walls. Maybe even a young professional or two thrown in—I glanced at the guy in square glasses and a plain white t-shirt. The room was low-lit and drowning in throws. Records were tacked to the walls, and an album was whirring in the corner. Some kind of chilled out hip-hop. I used to think it was *hip-pop* and I blushed very subtly.

"D'you wanna beer?" Julie loped back in, holding out a bottle to me before settling next to a girl with long, kinked hair that floated out from her head like a skirt. In it she wore a silver ribbon. In fact, everything she wore was silver. She suckled a vape. "This is Saiga." They sat close but that wasn't an indication of anything.

62

You could suck someone off in here, then ask for a cigarette and think nothing more of it. I remember that from uni. I remember the worst thing to do was think anything was a big deal. And squeezed into her Triumph Herald, she'd showed me what real abandon had looked like.

"Should you be doing that and driving... literally at the same time?" I asked her.

She smiled at me with her shining, prismatic face. Held out the bag for me.

"Imagine. All those many thousands of tuition pounds, wasted." The smoke suspended for a moment above her dark lipstick like a moustache, before being whipped out of the window.

"Oh what a waste!" I cried.

"She had so much potential!" We tipped our heads back and laughed into the star-studded night. Us against the world.

I leaned forward into the city lights. Imagine. All over the windscreen of a smashed-up car with her beautiful artist girlfriend...

"...if you're thinking of the antelope that recently inhabited a small region of the Eurasian steppe—" Saiga pulled me back from her wild driving "—you're right."

I wasn't.

"...and if you didn't know that they recently went extinct, you'd be like ninety percent of the world." She looked at me from beneath silver lids, drawing deep and releasing a voluminous cloud of sweet-scented water vapour. Lemon drizzle maybe.

"No, I didn't know that," I said, popping off the bottle cap with my molars like it wasn't the bravest thing a white girl could do. I sat cross-legged on a damp cushion. The guy next to me had a thick beard, but an unusually watery voice to back it up.

"Man, there's a bottle opener right there." He pointed at the vintage pine chest in the centre of the room, strewn with sketches, magazines, and books. *Fahrenheit 451* and Faulkner. Right.

"Ah, nae bother," I flipped my hand, swilling the broken shreds of tooth around in my mouth. Why was I being Scottish? "Nothing like a bit of extra calcium, eh."

A thin guy hooked up to a PlayStation in the corner spoke up. "You know it's a total myth created by the dairy industry that cows' milk strengthens your bones, whereas it *actually* leeches all the calcium *out of* your bones, causing them to—"

"Dolce," Julie cut across, "can generate a random vegan fact based on any one of millions of unrelated voice cues—" the guy's mouth closed like a lift "—and beardy over there is Jimmy. Poor Jimmy."

"So, you're all artists?" I asked, trying to lounge casually.

"Yeah basically," said Julie. "Well, trying." She grinned wide; a sudden, easy smile, as though she was the brightest gal in the world. A little ray of sunshine. "Saiga works in sculpture, Dolce does... Dolce kinda defies genre, don'tcha Dolce?" She turned slowly round to face him, pushing her hair around her face like a child smudging paint. Dolce was completely still, bar the twitching of his fingers on the controls and his lift-mouth.

"I'm taking one object at a time and tracing its entire production life. The origins of every aspect, it's movement throughout the world as it was forged from raw materials, through its manufacture, shipping; right down to its final resting place here, in our studio."

"Wow," I said. "That must take forever."

He let out a small sigh. "That's the point. Instead of just mindlessly consuming, I'm consuming *mindfully*." He paused. "It's basically meditation."

"Wouldn't it be better to not consume at all?" I asked, finishing my beer and grabbing another from the warm collection on the table.

Dolce barked at the screen: "If you think that's possible then I feel sorry for you." His eyes never left his avatar.

"So, what are you working on at the minute?" I asked.

"Well, I've done all my mugs. Next is cups."

"Bet that PlayStation will take you a bit longer." He didn't look round, but Julie did.

After my internment at home, it was good to be back. My new flat came with a TV. So retro. It felt nice to watch, like I was connected to something bigger, to all the others watching this never-ending news channel. Probably no one under 75. Eva was smoking a thick, white straight out the window, but the fumes rolled back in on the wintery air. She picked a 'pimple' on her calf.

"You should totally apply. Everyone at the firm is really nice, very friendly. The work is not so hard, and the money is goooooood." Eva elongated the sound and I smiled at her. When she tried to say 'wood' it came out like 'good,' and she emphasised the sound now for a shared comedic connection.

"Thanks Eva, but I'm just not really into the whole corporate thing. I want to get back into my art." On TV, I watched the Pope bless a baby through Skype. He must have had an upgrade to be able to access souls through digital media. Eva chewed her nails. She had honey-blonde hair ("Northern Spain, darling," Mum crooned) and eyes blue like. I pondered, turning my head to regard her the better. Zombie flesh.

Eva paused, biting her lip. "But your mother, she doesn't want you to do this art again, no?"

I exhaled. Eva was a nice girl, but you could tell she'd never disobeyed a parent *in her life*.

"Making art is all we can do to try and expose the all-invasive modes of late-capitalism," I said, sticking out my chin like I would at the barista. I hoisted myself off the sofa and towards the hall.

"But at uni last year, you got yourself into a terrible state when you hanged around with that strange woman did you no—" I clicked the door to my room shut. Fucking Eva.

I stood for a minute in the dim, looking over at the figure standing beside my bed. I switched on the light and moved past my as yet unchanged succulent collection, over to the beginnings of my next piece. The first since I'd dropped out of uni and returned home for my 'period of convalescence' ("Time to switch off, get out of your head for a bit!" Mum had said brightly on the way home from the hospital, with a gritted smile and a face so balled up the tears ran sideways off her face, like she was going a thousand miles an hour. In fact, she would never speed. No wonder I went to her. I had a need for speed. Haha).

The figure was about waist-high; still just a wire skeleton. I moved to the bedroom sink, the only good thing about this flat, and rolled up my oversized threadbare sleeves (£2 in the charity shop *and* I was doing good. They smelt like old stranger.) This would get Julie's attention. "I'ma coming for you Paula Heinz-beans!" I called out. "Or whatever your name is." I went to get a hairband. Inside, I touched the clippings of dark hair softly.

Closing the drawer, I pulled my hair up into a loose knot, pulling the hairband from my wrist round it, glancing in the mirror to pull down a few strands on either side of my face to make it *super* caj. Like Julie's hair. Julie's hair always looked so *caj* and started kneading water into the block of clay squatting in the sink.

I slept late, but I was up late. Working on *The Army*. The name drifted through my mind like a shell in shallow water. Figures of inert, grey clay, holding minds glittering with ideas. The head of each figure would have a cavity, filled with quartz. The mob awaiting mobilisation.

I checked my phone. 1pm. Fuck's sake. (Three missed calls from Mum. A text sent at 7am. Before she went to work. How did she do it. 'Eva said you were up late. Have you started looking for jobs? X'. I knew Eva was a dirty spy. Mum was obviously not relinquishing her role as acting-therapist; back at home in the provinces, NHS psychological services had all but completely withdrawn, along with every other arm of government spending. It was like international waters down there.)

In the kitchen, I opened up the bald heads of two organic eggs. Her shoulders had been speckled with freckles like these eggs. She had worn tiny, cropped tank tops, had worn one that day. She was that type of starved-skinny that everyone professed to hate now but really no one ever stopped thinking looked cool. For a minute I allowed small details of her to come back to me as I stood in the kitchen, yolk trickling down my arm.

She had whispers of silver at the roots of her long, dark hair. It was that obstinate brown that refused all warm tones: she

66

used to sprinkle it in her paintings and you never could pick it out from the huge black canvases. Her eyes were the same, her pupils and irises sinking into twin vantablack pots. Beyond that, not much of a looker. And despite her revolutionary ideas, she wasn't going anywhere.

In the end, she was just too dark in the head. I dropped the yolk-wet egg scalp into the sink.

Julie had said *Come by whenever.* I stopped at CULT and ordered my usual (for the first time) and waited for the good-looking barista to take notice. He handed me the drink with no smile and a "Cheers" so laid-back it was horizontal.

It was sunny out, with a stiff wind. I walked by the canal. A couple sitting on a bench threw breadcrumbs, which blew straight into the water. The pigeons didn't stand a chance.

It took ages for someone to answer the door. It was painted a dark blue (yes, rotting zombie flesh) with three tiny, diamond-shaped windows in a line down the middle. I pushed my face into the middle one, trying to peer through. Let me in.

The door swung open, and Saiga was standing there, silver spaghetti dress over glowing brown skin, flaking doc-martens on her feet; rollie stuffed behind her ear. "Oh, hey," she said, standing with one arm at the top of the door. Her armpit hair made me want to fall to my knees.

"Hey... how's it going?" I said.

"Pretty good, pretty good." She squinted at me, not moving.

I licked my lips. They were sore; Julie had clued me in on Vaseline's affair with Palm Oil.

"Is Julie in?" I asked slowly; I knew they could smell desire, that burning desire to 'hang out.' I must appear at all times nonchalant and vaguely absent. I kept my eyes half-closed and my phone in my hand. Julie was my passport back into this tangled undergrowth.

"She's out," said Saiga. Out before 2pm. I knew she'd be a great addition to The Army. Maybe a leader even. Her quartz would be the brightest. "What do you want?" Saiga asked. It wasn't rude, no—just straight up. Yeah, I liked straight up. No bullshit. "I'm working."

"What are you working on?" I said, perhaps an octave too high. With a tempo too quick. Perhaps.

She sighed and turned on her heel, leaving the heavy door ajar, "You can wait for Julie in here." I scrambled up into the hall. I could smell weed.

I followed Saiga into the main room. It must be perpetually dark in here. I tripped over a hunk of human flesh. "Oops, sorry," I mumbled, flushing at the growled 'fuck sakes' rising from the sleeping forms like smoke.

"We had a bit of a thing here last night," said Saiga, stepping gracefully in the gaps, just like her namesake (once did). I felt a sting at the non-invitation. I could have come, what did I do all night? Work on that stupid, fucking army, what a waste—

("What a terrible waste!" They would've wailed around the car wreckage, my mum whirling round with a box of tissues in each hand. "She was so clever, so much potential!")

"No worries," I said in reply to a non-existent apology, and raised a hand in greeting to the meek wave Jimmy was offering from a mound of shirtless torsos by the window. He was bleary-eyed and had a cigarette hanging from his lip. "Hey," he croaked. Poor Jimmy. I followed Saiga out of the room.

A corridor fed doors off on its right side. She pushed hard on the second one, and it made a noise like two freshly painted surfaces clacking apart. Once in, she coiled round the door behind me and pushed it shut. She was biting her lip.

Okay, her studio was genuinely cool. It was a white cube suspended over the canal, the far wall wholly glass. Hardly the open ocean of motivation posters, but brown water lapping moss-covered bricks was so much grimier, more real. Pushed against the walls were steep-sided mounds of rubbish, and filling the space in the middle were her own wire figures. "Hey, I'm doing something with figures too at the moment." I turned back to her, but she was looking down at her phone, arm crossed over her chest.

Not a problem. She'd listen soon enough.

Her figures were life-size and trapped between the wire was more rubbish. There must have been twenty-five of them. I know because I counted them. They cut twisted silhouettes against the bleak, white light of the early afternoon.

I turned back to her. "Very cool. What's your inspiration?" I asked.

"Well... people are just rubbish, aren't they?" she replied, her eyes translucent.

Back in the sitting room, the sleeping creatives had risen and were lounging about, speechless at their hangover. PlayStation guy screwed himself in, and Jimmy made tea. I stood around awkwardly, but then Julie came in. Thank gawd. She was breathless and it was so good to see her. I felt the fist inside me unfurl and I lurched forward, forgetting momentarily how uncool it was to smile.

"Aww hey man!" she said, offering a hi-five. I stared at her elbow and smashed her hand so hard I thought I would burst. "Whatcha doing here?" Her eyes glimmered. Her lids were less oily today. Cooling matt grey.

"Oh, Saiga was just showing me her sculptures," I gestured to Saiga, who had rescinded into shadow, becoming a glint of silver through her cloud of smoke.

"N'awww," Julie drawled, and hopped over to plant a kiss on her forehead. Saiga purred. My own forehead burned. "You're lucky, she almost never shows anyone her work. Saiga here is the most political of us all, our own little Paula Hursthein," Julie nodded back to me with enthusiasm. "When she dies, she's gonna have her body shipped off to sub-Saharan Africa to feed the poor. They're really not doing well over there," she said gravely.

"Oh yeah, very cool," I nodded, same tempo, same trajectory. Not too hard.

We stood there. There was a pause and I waited in it. I let it swell until she popped it. Would she pop it? Most people *hate* silence but that's because they're uncomfortable, unconfident, but Julie—

"Wanna see my stuff?"

Julie wasn't so different, really.

We stepped into her studio. Which was actually her bedroom if the mattress and tangled sheets were anything to go on. Tibetan prayer flags criss-crossed the ceiling, and the air was thick with old layers of incense. Julie knelt before a small workbench, as though in prayer. I settled next to her, trying to make as little sound as possible. Respect the practice.

On it were lined up little wooden figures. They were not quite human. One had two legs, but wings and a fish head, and also horns. Another was a snake with eyes growing on stalks all along its back. Strange half-human, half-animal hybrids. They were varnished and painted in bright colours, spots and stripes. She fingered one; it was about the size of her hand.

"What are they?" I asked, stitching my voice with the right strain of wonder.

"They're called Alebrijes. Traditionally made in Oaxaca, Mexico. They represent creatures you see in your dreams." She paused. "Traditional craftsmen believe they will protect you, that seeing them in your sleep is... like an omen, and if you bring them into the world of the wakefulness, you can nullify their power to haunt you."

My own dreams flashed in my head. The car skidding; the blood; her thin and angular corpse.

The waste, the terrible waste.

"D'you think you could extract things from other people's dreams?" I looked up from the red and yellow lizard-eagle hybrid I was holding, meeting Julie's eyes. Seaglass. My sexuality was fluid, sure.

"Oh definitely!" she nodded. "There's this lady on Fore Street who's commissioned me to model her Alebrijes. She wants to give them out as party favours at her next event. Paying me a bomb." She managed to keep a straight face.

"They're amazing," I mumbled. "I'm trying something out with dreams at the minute." I put the figurine back. It wobbled on uncertainly carved feet. Julie looked at me.

"You create?" she asked. Finally.

"I do," I said, my eyes moistening.

"What do you dream about?" Julie asked me. Her eyes were so clear, glassy pools beneath undercooked lids. I almost wet myself.

"It's not so much a dream... more like a vision I have." Julie nodded vigorously, urging me on. I spoke quickly. "I have this idea that there are these people—people like you, and me, and Saiga, and everyone, who *know* what's going on, who can tell that the late-capitalist structures make up an all-pervasive system that we cannot escape—like what PlayStation guy was saying, right? And all these people, us, we know this, and we just get along, right? But then, one day, when the revolution comes, we'll all be activated. We're out there, and we're just waiting for it. Like sleeper agents." I was breathless. I hadn't been allowed to talk like this since I left uni. Since my brain got scrambled by her, but I'm alright now, and Julie was nodding; I'd found them, my people. "I watched the Broadcast," I finished shyly.

Julie was staring at me. "It's amazing, isn't it?" she said, slowly. "I know, you're totally right by the way. I know exactly what you mean." There was a shade of respect in her eyes. A parasol erected by the pool. "The world is so crazy right now, and it's up to art to reveal that." She pushed her hand into her hair, looking around at her figures. "That's what Paula Heinsherst does so well; her pieces are the classic protests against all the fucked-up shit that goes on." Her voice took on that slight American twinge that happens when British people say things like 'fucked-up shit.' She nodded slowly, rocking her chin back and forwards slightly like a rocking horse. "A true radical."

I licked my lips.

Do I say: 'I have an uneasy relationship to art because on one hand I believe it has the power to change the world but on the other it's all just surface layer bullshit and my frustration between these two things once drove me into the arms of nihilistic madwoman but I just can't seem to stay away'?

Do I say: 'When I got too close to art last time, I ended up in a co-dependent relationship with a speed addict who framed her reckless abandon as a mega-conceptual performance piece that she claimed revealed the fragilities of all moral, ethical, and intellectual frameworks by which we purport to live our lives?'

Do I say: 'Help me find who I really am'?

Instead, I offered, "I watched the Pope bless a baby through a phone the other day."

"I know man, it's insane," Julie said, shaking her head in disbelief. She started rolling a joint.

"Right?" I replied, relieved at the levity. Keep it going. Hold her a little longer. I'll tell her soon enough. "I mean, how can you get access to someone's soul through a digital medium?" Julie smirked as she concentrated downwards. "Although I think I did get an STI through phone sex once," I finished, drolly. This elicited a tiny chuckle. I'd never felt so alive.

I began visiting Julie's place most days. Saiga puffed at me in resentful silence, but Julie really got me. We smoked Michelin-starred sativa. She cut my fringe, jagged like hers. Mum threatened to cut me off unless I started "seriously seeking work," but I said she sounded more like a claimants officer than a mother and that shut her up.

I was still in mourning—these things take time. But Julie was helping me reconnect, retune to the important stuff in the world again. The big issues. We spoke about the colonial legacy and the genocide that is the meat industry and the microplastics in the sea. She was helping me reboot my brain, giving me things to believe in again. She showed me that artists are the important voices representing these issues, introduced me to friends in galleries with dark lipstick and shaved heads. My breath clouded the screen of her phone.

At home, Eva hung about the door frame looking forlorn with her beautiful olive skin. I didn't want to be part of her corporate bullshit world. "You don't even know what you *do*," I sneered at her one evening.

"And you don't know that you're sick," she said, tears brimming. "You made up all that shit with that woman, you're just a delusional girl with no—"

I slammed the door again and again, making the figures of The Army shake. The succulents stayed turgid and I glared at them as I puffed to the sink, ripped apart the clay. I pulled off my shirt and smeared clay on my body. I was one of them, one of them. One day, Julie and I would show everyone the truth.

"Guys guys guys! You won't believe this." Julie sat up straight, clutching her phone in front of her face, Saiga slumping in the empty space she left. "Paula. Heinshurst. I think she's doing a secret show."

"What?!" Everyone jumped up and rushed to crowd around Julie's phone. She was spluttering.

"Look! So, you know she posted that Hushed Cow album yesterday, well, then in *their* tour notes there's a reference to The Broadcast, and they're playing in the Boiling Room on Tuesday..." I zoned out, watching Julie pin together the clues like a beautiful detective. The others hopped in slow-motion around her. PlayStation face continued to play.

"Friday night. She's doing a performance." Julie's face looked numb. "She's the whole reason I got into art."

Everyone fell back into their places.

"That is actually crazy though; I thought she'd completely lost it?" said PlayStation guy

"Nah, nah, she went off the rails in the early 2000's but she's been doing much better since her suicide," said Julie.

"Don't you mean suicide attempt?" I asked.

"Paula Hienshurts doesn't *attempt* anything," Saiga snorted from within her smoke cloud like a grumpy genie. I'd obviously rubbed her the wrong way. Haha. "She *gets. Shit. Done.*"

Julie stayed staring at her phone. "Alright Saiga, cut it out."

Saiga fell silent.

I held my breath.

Then she gathered together her limbs and stalked off through the mess of the living room. The curtains were drawn against the day, but the sunlight cut through the darkness in long, columns of swirling dust, and her scowl flashed at me as she passed through each one.

I stared at the hole by Julie's side. I was about to move into it, take my rightful place, her right-hand woman (but on her left for now), but then Poor Jimmy wandered over and settled down next to me. Well, now it would look rude. He pulled a smooth white pebble out of his pocket and began to rub it, staring at it insistently.

"What are you doing?" I asked.

"I consider the pebble. Helps me smooth out my wrinkled brain, you know?"

I wanted to grab his hand. "I know."

I let myself into the flat quietly. I didn't want to see Eva. We hadn't spoken since our blow-out the other day. I had forgiven her—her job must be so spiritually draining, knowing how much she was contributing to everything that was wrong with the world. And she'd pay when the time came.

I moved into my room. The Army of figures was almost finished. Julie would come over to see them soon. I just needed to source the quartz and I'd be all done. I smoothed down the rough fringe of the tallest one—it'd been hard to sprinkle the dark hair in, but it was time to move on—and tweaked the silver dress of another. No matter how I'd twisted the clay on that one, she'd still come out with a willowy grace it was hard to ignore. At least the silver had been dulled to grey. And when the revolution happened we would all rise to the call together, and crush the automatons who stood in our way, too stupid to realise the revolution was here. Even her. Her big, dark brain would be crushed, smeared all over the walls.

I looked at the grey clay stain.

That's all she would ever be.

Paula was having her comeback in a church, at midnight. Church-cum-café-cum-barbershop-cum-vegan-cooperative. Cum cum cum. I opened a beer. She had made me cum. What was so wrong with that? Eva had cocked an eyebrow when I'd first told her about

Gloria. "Maybe she made you feel free, like with no trouble in the whole world." Eva smiled coquettishly. "I can see your appeal. But she wasn't good for you either. She was so dark and gloomy. And wasn't she really old?" They had been working together, her and Mum, this whole time. In cahoots. The thought swirled around in my mind.

I came out of my room at 11:10, with plenty of time for once. I locked my door and turned around to face Eva, and Mum. I blinked.

"What are you doing here?" I asked.

"Darling, I'm just worried about you." Mum sighed, stalking into the kitchen. Did she expect me to trail after her? I trailed after her. Eva trailed after me.

"Eva tells me you've been acting odd, hanging out with some scummy artists—again." I looked at her from beneath my oily lids. "There is no need to get bogged down in all that again now, is there sweetie? This is meant to be you starting your life again, making something of that fantastic little brain of yours!" Her face crinkled; she looked older than she felt. "It's time to forget all about that horrible druggie and concentrate on succeeding, okay?"

I stood there, puffing steam like a bull whilst she extracted mugs from the cupboard, tea from the box, milk from the fridge and filled the kettle, all at once, with her multi-fucking-tudinous arms. Enough.

"How can you speak of the dead like that?" I thundered.

She leant against the kitchen side, clasping her hands in front of her.

"Listen, honey. You know, that day, in the car..." I could see where she was going with this, yet again, why did she refuse to acknowledge the truth and I stamped my foot and let out a little screech. Eva jumped slightly in the corner, hand folded over her mouth like she was in a fucking soap.

"Mum!"

"Everyone was fine, nothing happened; no one was *killed—*"

I clamped my hands over my ears and got down into a low squatting position, squeezing my eyes shut. "Mum, I'm not listening to this bullshit again..."

"She wasn't healthy for you, she screwed with your head! Putting in all sorts of ideas in there, putting all sorts of things up your nose as well..." she scoffed.

Eva piped up through her soggy face. "You know you say to me, I know, this woman, she helps you forget the world, makes you think nothing matters, and she makes you feel goooooooood—" I thumped the cupboard and a mug tipped off and smashed on the tiles. This time they both jumped silent. I stood up, breathing hard.

"No! I will not listen to this!" I shouted. "You have no idea how hard it's been for me Mum, you know, and frankly Eva," I whirled to hiss in her face, "you should stay out of it, you don't know *what* happened—"

"Eva told me you're still deluded about what happened!" Mum suddenly screeched. "There was no crash that day, okay? Gloria didn't die in a car crash, and as much as you fantasise about it, neither did you!"

I turned on my heel and made for the door. I wasn't listening to any more of this *shit*. I could hear her following me down the hall.

"Look, I know it's some sick thing for you, to fantasise about 'dying too young', like some tortured artistic soul, oh, what a waste it would've been, and d'you know what—" I opened the door, but she grabbed my shoulder and spun me round to face her "—it would've been." Her face was screwed up, her eyes scanning me. "She saw that sickness in you that day you grabbed the wheel and, quite rightly, called me to come and take you home."

"Stop it! Stop fucking lying to me!" I screamed in her face, trying to wrest myself free but she gripped my upper arms in her bony fingers.

"I'm not *fucking* lying to you!" she hissed the profanity up close to my face. "You need to accept the facts; you have *got* to stop this self-delusion—" Images started flashing through my head.

The car screeched off the corner, jumped the ditch, smashing into the gatepost—

"Mum, no—" My eyes closed as she shook me.

76

—my seat belt cutting into my shoulder, a horizontal rain of glass glinting in the sunlight—

"You have to come to terms with it—"

—her brains skewered on the jagged edges of windscreen—

She was shouting now, "Having Gloria die makes it all a lot easier, doesn't it? Rather than accepting what really happened—" I started to go limp in her arms, but she propped me up like a doll.

—blood soaking my clothes, her intestines sliding off the dashboard—

All that whirling had paid off; her grip was steel-tight.

—curling around the wheel like they wanted to drive us away from it all—

"She was never your girlfriend," Mum's voice cracked in the middle, like an urn. Ashes whispering through the gap like smoky water. "She asked you to leave her alone—"

—and her tiny corpse slumped like roadkill on the bonnet—

"No!" I shut it down. "Let go of me!" It was meant to be hard and assertive, but the cry seeped out of me in a squeal. I twisted myself down and out of her grip and she moved her arms away. I lurched towards the still-open door. What must the neighbours think?

I looked back at her, I know I should've kept my eyes straight ahead, but I looked back at her, just for a second; just to see her slumped form and sagging face. It looked like a brown paper bag—like one you might breathe into during a panic attack. Eva was moving in for a hug; probably a lovely, warm, sunny-honey, I'ma-so-funny Spanish hug. That fucking traitor.

I wiped my nose and turned out into the night.

By midnight the city was already drunk. I was already drunk. To my left, a girl in a tiny, tiny dress, (did she really think that looked good?) stepped back, tripped over, fell into a metal barrier that collapsed under her puppy-weight. I caught the look of indignation in her eyes as she fell back. I knew that look, had once looked that look. The girl burst into tears on the floor, and a bouncer in a hi-vis left his post and hurried over to go above and beyond. I walked on. The Army would walk on.

"WHY WON'T HE REPLLYYYYYYY," I heard her squealing from the dark behind me and I winced, remembering the squeal I had made at mum. She always used to say, "I know when you're telling porkies because you squeal like a pig." I should've replied in emotionless monotone, like Julie. Grey-lidded Julie. She was the clay around my quartz. She was my encasement, carrying me along.

I turned the corner, narrowly avoiding a pile of sick. I looked up the street and saw that piles of it continued in short, sharp bursts all the way to the end. They obviously had a lot to get out. I knew that feeling too. I staggered slightly and clutched the wall. An empty white wine bottle with a pink straw protruding from it sat next to an ATM, acting as though it wasn't totally responsible for the carnage wreaked all around. The Supreme Overlord of Saturday Night.

I met everyone outside the red-lit entrance. They stood at the edge of a huge crowd waiting for the venue to open. Julie, Saiga, PlayStation and Poor, Poor Jimmy.

"I can't believe I'm getting to see Paula Heinsherst. This is a real dream come true," Julie buzzed. Saiga had her arm around her. They'd obviously made up. Saiga was wearing dark purple lipstick. Why didn't I think of that?

I guess I'd been a little distracted. Mum's face loomed in my mind again, and I tried to strangle her as before, but she morphed and melted through the axons like wax. The drink was putting off my aim. Weakening my grip. Julie reached out and steadied me by the arm. I gave her a hopeless smile. I opened my mouth to say,

"Come and lead the Army with me," or something else inappropriately sincere, but then the doors opened, and everyone poured in.

I tried to stay as close as I could to Julie as we pushed through to the front of the crowd, towards a small stage. My brain was fizzing and I needed my cooling clay, her balming, effortless conviction. It was hot and I regretted wearing tights. I glanced down at Saiga's effortlessly bare legs. Just skin. So cool.

The red space suddenly flashed black, and everyone turned down their volumes. I tried to focus my eyes. A white spotlight came on, illuminating a table and two chairs on the stage.

"I can't see," Saiga whispered.

PlayStation tilted his head down to her, "There's a table, and two chairs. The table has a red and white checkered tablecloth, two plates, an arrangement of cutlery—"

"So, just two place settings?" Julie cut across.

PlayStation rolled his eyes. "I'm trying to see things in a particulate way. It has a candle dripping wax predominantly on its left side—"

"Will you shut up, there she is!" Julie squeaked.

From the dark of the wings there appeared an impossibly thin woman. It jolted me. Her face was lined, but her hair cropped short and dyed peroxide blonde. What if it wasn't dyed?

She moved like an eel through dappled water and settled down on one of the chairs. She faced the audience and now I could see she had a large, red smile painted clown-like across her round face. I exhaled.

"Well, I sure am hungry, I hope my date arrives soon." Her American accent was rolled into plasticine sausages. "Oh, here he comes now." A tall man wearing a rubber, Ken-doll mask appeared and joined her at the table. "What do you fancy, honey?" she asked.

"Honey?" he boomed back, looking out into the lights. "No, I'm sweet enough." A strange, warbled screaming sound dragged through the air.

"That's the backwards laughing track," Julie whispered, transfixed. "They used it in The Broadcast." I nodded back vigorously. She didn't look at me.

"Well, I'm *trying* to be vegetarian," the thin woman said, tracing a finger down a piece of cardboard. A menu board. "But since *you're here*, I'm gonna have a burger." She put her menu down and stared back at the man. Her upper lip was wet.

"Nothing wrong with that. Treat yourself!" the man said.

Paula leaned into the audience with her hand cupped around her mouth, and I felt the crowd around me lean forward to greet her in one collective move. "Except I also had one yesterday, sacrificial slaughter to The Hangover." She winked, and an actual laugh rippled through the crowd. Julie's face was opened up into the widest, sloppiest grin I'd ever seen on her.

Paula then stood up and took on a dramatic pose. "Yes. I deserve it. Day after day I wave them by, those phantom barnyard animals." A projector whirred on, and white holograms of cows, pigs, and chickens moved robotically along the stage. "You shall not be eaten today my friends. You may go straight into the children's books. But today, yes, a burger would be *perfect*. Just what I *fancy*." She sat down again. Ken-man laughed like a tin can full of coins.

"Well then, this restaurant may be a new kind of experience for you." To the right side, a long, lowing moan pushed through the curtains. Ken stood up to greet the calf as it lumbered onto the stage. When it reached him, he stroked it under its russet chin. "Here, you know *exactly* where your food is coming from."

Beside me Julie took a sharp breath. "I can't believe they're actually doing it."

Doing what. I swayed slightly on my feet.

Ken and the thin woman moved to either end of the animal, crouching down to hoof level. They bound the ankles together. then they grabbed them and yanked the back and front legs in opposite directions. The calf screamed. Stretched out the middle. Waves of heat were steaming off the crowd.

Stress-sweat.

Ken looked out at the audience, "This is all about *experiencing* the death we love the taste of so much." Paula's eyes looked stony as she pulled. Like clay.

Suddenly, somehow, the calf snapped; and the air ruptured. The skin burst and blood volcanoed out, and the calf died with a terrible, guttural sob. Organs slimed onto the stage with a sound like someone throwing up and the crowd erupted into a bedlam of cries and screams. Beside me, Julie retched and turned her face into Saiga's shoulder.

"Omg, omg, omg," she was whispering. Why was she looking away? She was meant to be all about facing the truth. I turned back to the stage, annoyed. The artists had got onto their hands and knees and were lapping the blood. Behind the artists you could see two large metal pulleys.

"How about some smoky bacon on top?" asked Ken, his mask soaked red.

"How can they do this?" Jimmy whispered to me, and I leaned back to explain, breathlessly:

"They didn't actually snap it with their brute force—see, there's like two metal pulley systems behind them..." He was looking at me with a twisted face. "Bit gimmicky, but gotta be done for the effect eh," I finished, my eyes dragging me back into the scene. I was totally absorbed, giddy with excitement. This was it. This was art showing the truth. The activation. Paula Heinz-beans was a genius! I soaked up the blood with my eyes. Yes. This could work.

The images flooded in with the blood from the stage. Her body—

—soaked with blood—

A squealing pig went scrabbling across the stage.

*—*my mum swooped in: *"Don't tell porkies darling"—*

The soft, white down between the pig's shoulders glinted in the spotlight.

—her freckled shoulders, my beautiful Gloria, my Glorious Gloria—

Paula leant across and caught the pig, her fist closing around its hoof. "I can already see the fat bubbling between his shoulders," she cackled hysterically. "I love knowing where my food comes from." She pulled out a scalpel and it flashed in the spotlight like windscreen glass. It was all starting to come together.

"I can't watch this, this is barbaric," said someone next to me.

Someone else whined, "She's gone too far this time." I felt space opening up in the crowd around me as people began to leave. Finally, some air. The ones who lingered were shouting; booing and hissing like this was some sort of pantomime instead of the truth; the call.

Finally. The call.

I stared, transfixed. "Susie, c'mon." I felt a pull on my arm and I snapped out of my daze, turning to see Julie's pale face amongst the crowd, flashing in the lights—on the stage they'd flicked on a strobe and were dancing in the entrails. Julie was staring at me, eyes filled with panic. The crowd lurched around us, riptides pulling in opposing directions. Now that I looked round, I saw that lots of people were crying. Other faces were distorted with anger and disgust, and some people had started lobbing things onto the stage.

"We can't just leave," I said, pulling her back in to me. "Julie, *this* is it. Leaving would reveal us for the hypocrites we are. If we really are committed to fighting the system, we should be up there with them! They're just showing us what happens behind closed doors, behind the sanitised doors of slaughterhouses—" Julie looked from me up to the stage. I turned to look as well and saw Paula Heins-beanz doing the worm through the carcasses. "Okay, so maybe not *exactly* what's going on in slaughterhouses," I conceded. Julie was backing away, shaking her head. "The western world can't handle their own realities!" I laugh-shouted as she turned and ran out. I could hear the wail of police sirens in the distance.

Screw her then. I didn't need Julie or her stupid antelope-girlfriend. I moved to the barrier, hoisting myself up and over. Security was at the exit, clambering over one another to get out. Silly piggies. I climbed up onto the stage, a beer bottle whistling past my ear and smashing somewhere off to the right. Bad aim. Bad steering.

I dropped to my knees in the blood. Maybe filling the hollow heads of The Army with quartz wasn't the best representation. I'd wanted to have something solid and precious, twinkling unassumedly. But when the call for change came, what would make people sit up and take notice? Maybe blood would be better. I drew Her outline with my fingers. Blood changes things. It changed that day in the car, with Her. Freed me from Her. From Her airtight grip on me. That grey stain smeared on my wall—it wasn't enough. She was more than a smudge on my brain—She'd got into my circulatory system, tried to suck it dry.

I scooped up two cupped handfuls of organs and brought them close to my face. They could be Her. Maybe this is what I needed; this was the medium I needed for Her, to bring Her out, get Her out of me. Get those insides outside. In-out-in-out-shake-it-all-about. I draped a line of intestines over my shoulders like a feather boa and shimmied in time. Haha.

Other people had clambered up on the stage around me, but when I looked round, they weren't knee-deep in offal, rooting around in the carnage for answers. They were restraining the artists whilst police handcuffed them. Ah, probably a good thing really. There was too much death in this world without needlessly adding to it. Probably shouldn't hang around though—I started filling my pockets.

Her thin, twisted corpse, and my big, twisted brain.

In the end, neither were any good.

WASHED UP

The herd were moving through the storm-turned coastline when they found you, bobbing face up in one of the sheltered southern coves. Turned in by the current now bored with you. The storm coughed and rolled away, embarrassed.

The herd rose, full-form, like the muggy breath of upturned soil. They grew from the rockface and ballooned from bark and rubble lining the ripped rim of the cliff. They dropped into the milk-rose water around you on parachutes of plumed chatter.

The sky was half-open—either dawn or dusk. i remember the cajoling of fish-backs as they nudged you towards the shore. The herd gathered and the fish stayed. They tell me later that your face was so swollen with water, you must have been drifting for a long time.

The herd poked and prodded, then rolled you around like a sack of peaches. You did not stir. Your eyes were open but, when the herd tell me this story later, they call them unfilled graves.

Waist-high in spume, the herd whistled and called whilst the sea moved restlessly beyond the rocks. Yapping for you. So then tying themselves round you, the herd, and pulling you ashore. Logs and cans lurked in the whipped waters, bopped you on the head like drunk crocodiles. Small gangs of flies came from the black beach to escort the procession. There was a sound, and it could have been singing.

Noises puffed out of you, little gasps of structure that built out of your mouth before smoking away into the air. Your words didn't make sense here anymore.

Alien.

Inside, i remember you were staring into a hot mirror. It was ringed with lights. *Looking back at you, your massive grin, cracking your whole face. Tears streaming down each side and a panicked gurgle in your oesophagus. "Where's Mariana?"*

"What a beautiful smile." A voice, from before. Hard to hear amongst sirens and shaking. An easy, smiling face. Strapping you in. "You just keep focussing on that beautiful smile of yours."

You, trying to unclip the belts around your waist. "I want Mariana."

We remember the force. A star-glinted road. The voice, ringing amongst gases: "Focus on that smile. It will keep you whole."

You tried to somersault back, back to that smiley face, to Mariana, but the coordinates reversed, the glistening cave cracked, and out you slid, into a post-storm dawn/dusk beach of black sand and slick air and the calls of broken birds. The mushed-up yoke of you.

Your eyes refocused on the sky, nacreous pulp. A huge, black blur bifurcated your vision like a zip.

Is it a bird?

The words were there, suddenly, in your head. Not spoken. Without memory-scuffed edges, like the smiley face voice. Flat and bloodless, like a pre-recording. Then they were gone.

The herd gathered around you, kneeling in the hot, black sand, their voices marbling through the heavy air. They looked like bloody shapes to you, supermarket flesh. But you could feel them, rubbing your numb body. Pain glistened through you, like a photo dipped in developing fluid.

They kneaded you back in, they tell me, like bread. You were so cold, but not like sea in bloodstream nor the bones of moonlight.

86

More like an instant freezing when they touched you. Like their own bodies didn't exist; had never existed. The cold that precedes life.

Then, someone folded clarity in. The shapes solidified. You saw bodies, heads, faces... Sort of. The one closest to you, rubbing your arms, had huge, globular eyes that protruded from her face. Above your head, another face bobbed; inquisitive, symmetrical. But horizontally.

They were people.

Sort of.

Another push and your ears unfurled, sounds inflating and popping inside your light-filled head.

"Us-we must slap it!" said the one with globular eyes. You flinched. They could talk. "Let cries fill the valley! Dissect their meat."

Sort of.

The one above, massaging your temples, made a serrated sound. "That never works." Something fell from her mouth; a tongue, multi-tendrilled and tomia-flecked. It dangled over you, dropping spit on your face. "Us-we should take it to the woods and lick it clean. Its name will be written in cum." You wished you could move.

"Name!" huffed one down the bottom end, maybe the one pounding your heels. They leaned into your line of vision. They had a strong, arched nose and eyes crowded together at the top, like divers scared to jump. "Its *story* will be written in scalp braille."

"Will it, this time?" mumbled multi-tongue. Her tendrils explored your face independently.

Arched nose ignored this. "Let's engulf it. Us-we intestines can read it."

Things returned to you that you didn't know you'd lost. Your blood unfroze with screams as it began to flow. You remembered your skin, a line in the dust. You could feel the sand beneath you, hot and fluttering, a rhythmic beat through it. Footsteps.

A voice called from further away. "Us-we! What've you found?"

You knew that voice. From the before.

"Shit!" said multi-tongue. "Quick, give us suck before us-we rejoins."

You wanted to sit up, look for the voice, but there was a crack right through as your organs rediscovered you *GLORIOUS ORGANS:* your liver and your heart and a mulchy stomach, ringing with underuse.

The voice, closer. "Us-we! Another one? Washed up?" It sounded so familiar. "Wait. Wait. Is that...?" The footsteps sped up.

The herd rubbed faster, scooping out your pores. You remembered your anus and grinned. It was all rushing back now, flushing out the fractal structure that had deadened your body for so long. *"You won't feel a thing. It's all up here."* The smiley face. *"All in that pretty little head of yours."*

The footsteps on the sand stopped. "Oh my god. Us-we, where did you get that? Who is that?"

You shook your head free from the lights of before. Tried to refocus outwards, on that voice.

"It washed up," said multi-tongue. Her tendrils withdrew.

"Let me see!" The voice dropped down close to you.

You drew apart your fused mouth like wet tissue-paper. "Who."

It dribbled down your cheek like spittle, and mariana caught it on her finger.

She says it was the heaviest word she ever held.

Overlooking the scene on the black beach, the plants on the cliff and in the dunes cavorted with their insects, who were too drunk to care. Fruiting plants belched up heavy tangs of spores and dribbled nectar into the humid night air. The sky rotted. Amongst the entangled branches, others watched from their territories.

They sensed it too. This feeling, as though visited by a ghost.

i understand this now.

The herd helped you up, though even this was dizzying. You tried to focus, but the sea was dancing, and the birds were flying and even the sand was a pulsing, throaty growl.

"Head is not vine-embroidered like us-we," said arched nose, supporting you. "It will bob away again."

88

The one with the voice squatted over your legs, an arm on your shoulder. So close. "We have to move her from the beach."

Globular eyes turned to her.

"Us-we, i mean," said the voice. You tried to look at her face, but it was obscured by the before-light. "Move the beach from it." Globular's eyes sucked in and out wetly, like anemones. The voice continued. "It's too open here. The others will claim her. It."

"There are no others," said arched nose. They lifted a hand to you. "Head may be open like cave but has walls. See here, mineral lines? Scar tissue. Diddled with."

Arched nose touched you behind your ear and the bright lights inside your head suddenly switched off. You turned to see the voice's face but from the darkness in your head, rising to the surface, words began to appear, itching your mouth. They shot towards you, from all directions. *Smiley face tapping your temple.* "*Everything we ever knew has all been saved, stored right up here.*" These were your things, repopulating your head at breakneck speed, and then you were screaming, screaming before you even know what they meant. You shot up from the sand, eyes pulsing.

"*10 ways to enlarge your penis!*"

The herd stumbled back as one, crouching together.

"*You won't believe these celebrity nudes,*" you continued. "*44 Beatles facts to make you twist and shout.*"

"What is celebrity nudes?" anemone eyes whispered to mariana, but mariana crouched in on herself, skin folded. More was coming.

"*What they didn't teach you in school about these US presidents.*"

The herd laid arms on each other, humming as they watched you jerk up and down on the hinge of your hips.

"*Study says we start losing our friends after 25 and This company designed a tampon for mess-free period sex and Girls who have letter 'A' at the beginning or end of their name are the hardest to impress.*"

You stamped about the beach, spewing megabytal nothing. Your head peeled back over your body and that dazzling mirror of light flooded out.

Arched nose nodded. "Lost bones with no sinew-braiding."

The herd fanned out to surround you, to keep the water from taking you again. The one with the voice edged closer to you, arms up, fingers splayed. "Bea, it's me. It's me, mariana."

That name. From the before. You stumbled towards her, her face a pulsing bauble of light. You tried to talk: *"Are you alone? This game will make you cum in 15 seconds."* It's not what you wanted to say.

Night fell. A wind appeared, crouching on the cliff edge, breathing heavily. Another, then many, heaving with excitement. Cackling with dried bracken, they leapt up and down the rockface and around the herd and the strange creature, whipping up big black tails of sand like exhaust fumes. The herd closed in around you.

"Where is your herd?" they said.

"How do you love?"

"Singles in your area looking for love." You darted about, tracing your feet across the glitter-black. *"Use your chart to find your soulmate. Gemini and Aquarius are compatible intellectually. I am Gemini. I am Year of the Goat."* Your feet drew symbols in the sand, over and over. Your head snapped wildly, arms flapping like frustrated wings. *"I have brown hair and blue eyes. I like long walks on the beach and reading crime novels."*

Your outline was blurring again, your skin emitting a loud hum. The insects liked it and started to boogie.

"Make it stop!" said arched nose, covering their ears. "It's bursting at seams and they're not stitched!"

"You're no fun," said multi-tongue, twisting closer to you and flashing her tendrils at your translucent back. "Let's open it up, see what's inside!"

Mariana batted away the flickering prongs and turned in to you, hunched and dribbling in the sweaty dusk air. "Us-we, i know this," she said. "She is not body but headbrains. Her speak is something we cannot touch."

"Again? You never give them to us-we," growled anemone eyes.

"Not this one." Mariana looked down at you. "She – it will make us-we sick."

"Sick, healthy. These are your things." Multi-tongue looked bored. "Can't us-we just eat it and be done? It makes us-we dizzy."

You shuddered with sparks, a fit of psychic shitting. *"Democracy riots, the great floods, the Cassini spacecraft, help, smokestacks, four million teenagers, a wife gasping, a sea of plastic, an upturned palm tree, the valleys below, make them see there's no plan(et) b."* You were drowning in a shaken-up jigsaw. You bashed corners into holes, unable to create final beautiful picture of the end of the world. *Smiley face is no longer smiling. "You're our little golden disc." He seals you in.*

Mariana tried to shake you out of it, but when she touched you, your skin flaked away. The massage wasn't enough. "She needs your strength," said mariana to the herd. "Us-we, she needs growth and seed and mud-planting. This electric headbrains, it fries body and makes no smell."

Us-we replied, "The forest," though multi-tongue wasn't quite in time. She was high-stepping her long body around you, flicking tongues. Arched nose barked at her and she slithered away.

Together, the herd melted towards the dunes at one end of the beach, leaving you pacing up and down the sand. They followed mariana to the fat plants lining dunes' crest and into the undergrowth beyond, where it twists together and nothing is separate. She crawled through to the muggy earth, rubbing it on herself, through herself. Had to whisper the right words, she tells me later. Only then could she scoop a handful. Good, sweet earth.

Good, sweet earth, the herd murmur in unison.

Back on the beach, the darkening sky met with the black of the sand like a closing eyelid. You lay there. *Smiley face talking, but to someone else. "If the data is compromised, it'll sacrifice the organic casing to protect itself."* Your head swallowed you back up, eroding your body like a corpse in a vat of acid. Quantum mobsters dissolve the evidence.

The white glow from your eyes was the only light now on the beach now and the bugs crawled over them in delight. Moth party. Words steadily pulsed through you, and as you remembered you spoke them to no one. *'Algae blooms, Hollywood, tuna, wanna, sacrifice, tits, heteronormative, melting, wholesale subjugation and slaughter, polar bears, yes!, premium cocaine, microbeads, rape, drones, colonial settler, slavery, delivery, delete her, discourse, dead, dead, dead, dead...'*

You got stuck on this last one, the disc skipping. With each chant, a face appeared before you, mostly human, the odd dog and cat thrown in, but before you could hold each one, it was gone, replaced by another. Your hands clawed in front of you.

The herd returned to the beach. They stepped along the rivets, avoiding the burrows of sand-dwellers. The waves rubbed along the shore, purring.

"It's too quiet," said anemone eyes. The cove night-air was usually so thick with the trilling hopes and fears of night creatures that even their thoughts had to fight for space, let alone make speech. The herd took each other's wrists.

The dark was pregnant. Something else.

It swirled against the air, trying to escape, a smell they recognised from feeding. Like running into a gong, multi-tongue always says, with bared teeth.

You lay slumped in the shallows, eyes flashing on and off. Your body stuttered. Delicately, oh so gently, mariana shifted you down. She parted your legs and thrust her fistful of earth up inside you.

You thickened. The flashes of your eyes started to deepen in tone—stolen cream—golden arches—final orangutan—kiss-goodbye red, each flash illuminating dark shapes appearing on the beach around you, before the darkness swallowed them back up. Wet pops and squelches sounded through the night, sulfurous bubbles on the surface of a hot spring. Bursting forth from the skin of the air, highlighted for a second before fading again. Millions, stacking up in great piles along the beach, each flash showing more and more. The dead.

The herd knew these forms, but not in this number. They had this smell in their blood, but never this thick. The scent tugged at their stomachs and they began to growl, drawing them high in their throats. Mariana stood back and watched as the hunger swaddled the herd.

This was Death. But not its sneeze or tickle amongst sick or old. Not its wink as it offers prey. ·

"This is extinction," said mariana to the winds and they carried the word away, never knowing where to drop it.

Mariana looked at you, flashing in the water like a dying squid. When she tells me this later, she swallows. Lifts my foot to her face – in our time apart, we have developed different languages of comfort.

The lights in your head receded, leaving fluorescent burn marks on your vision. You got to your hands and knees *Now let's take a couple cat-cows* and looked around at the mounds of bodies. *Breathe deep.* Word-nets flashed from inside your drive and you draped them over.

"It's been named! 2001's scent of the year! Field after field of burning cows."

The pain was returning, roaring through you now.

"TWENTY-FIVE ANIMALS YOU DIDN'T KNOW WERE EXTINCT! 95% of the world is inhospitable for life other than crop. The boy washed up on the beach."

This was our body too, mariana says, licking tears off my face.

"He has been identified as Alan Kurdi."

You had lost something, but you didn't know what. You felt the loss, but you didn't know what.

Mariana moved around you, past the collective corpses and the feeding women. She tasted your pain. Jaw set grim, she cracked your head, and your eyes went dark.

bloodbitch

Mariana was gone.

You sat up in the warm foam of the tide's edge. It was dawn and the sun was whipping the sea red raw, but the water remained stoic, calm. Sliding past the headland was the hump of some great grey beast. It was hot already. Stinking. You heard a strange bird cry and, for the first time, you wondered where you were.

You turned and looked up the beach and saw that the herd *were still researching the aftereffects of mass extinction, emulated by dumping 3000 tonnes of dead pigs into the woods. Mass extinction occurs following a sudden and totalising environmental change and has very rarely been caught on camera. But the Mississippi experiment changes that, tracking the decomposition process, from the appearance of maggots and rats, through to top-chain scavengers such as vultures and armadillos. After eighteen months, there is still activity, including a dense forest of mushrooms that are edible themselves, completing a cycle—*

The horror! You hauled your meat away from them, crawling as fast as you could in the opposite direction, towards the dunes. At their fringe you could see thick fleshy plants and you remembered Mariana and the herd bringing dirt to you. You would find her. Find Mariana.

You managed to stand *Imagine a string pulling you up from the crown of your head,* but your feet unspooled in the shifting sand. The grains giggled. You nearly came slithering back down, but then they abandoned their watery tricks and helped you step to solid ground. You wobbled into the jungle *the mighty jungle.*

A gull enjoying the dawn from a passing seagarbage patch saw you hobbling up the black sand and shouted good luck.

You pushed your way into the undergrowth, feeling the sandy soil turn moist beneath your toes. "Good, sweet earth." This must be where Mariana went. You listened, but every sound was magnified: leaves falling, trees drinking, moss laughing. The six-beat rhythm of an ant's footsteps *I like all music, except jazz.* You combed through the cacophony for Mariana's voice. She was here, you were sure of it.

Neon labels projected out onto the plants and litter around you: *Sisyrinchium bermudiana, aluminium bauxite, Rhyncholaelia digbyana, Caesalpinia Pulcherrima, metalicised plastic film.* The outside drew red lines across your body and nicked your feet as you pushed past them, into the thickness. i remembered you start to panic, getting more and more entangled in the vines and the polymer. They were strapping you in, sealing you in, that smiley face smiling away, *"All in that pretty little head of yours,"* when you jolted forward into a clearing bathed in soft, red light. The vines withdrew with a hiss.

You stood in a perfect bite out of the vegetation: a pocket of hot, red air, like the inside of a mouth. Cautiously, carefully, you puffed out your own in greeting.

In the middle of the clearing, like a nucleus, you noticed a large, red lump. It was about as big as a *bean bag chair.* You circled around it, and decided yes, it could very well be this *bean bag chair* and you felt a strong magnetic pull to collapse onto it and *Play next episode?* However, peering closer to it... No, you didn't recall that same throbbing coming from a *bean bag chair.* Or those slurping noises? And did they ooze out a dark, glutinous liquid?

You heard rustles from behind and you pulled your new skin in tight around you like a cloak *lions and tigers and bears.* Was it the herd? They had come back for you. They'd eaten your loss-I-don't-know-what and now they were back for you, for their freshly kneaded bodydough. You took a step backward but now the sound was behind, and you whipped round to face a small person crouched over the pulsing *bean bag chair.*

It wasn't one from the herd. She was smaller, though it was hard to tell with the *bean bag chair* obscuring most of her body. Only

95

her head was visible, her face close to the lump. Her little black eyes were fixed *Press Left trigger to lock on* you while she whispered furiously to the *bean bag chair,* little bits of spittle escaping her mouth. The lump quivered and throbbed, emitting a low-frequency warble. All the while, she caressed it with her palms, sliding them over its veiny surface. Your head started flicking through images at a billion results per second, trying to track it, trap it, eat it, burn it *animal vegetable or mineral* but it kept wriggling free.

"My big juicy one... i love you, i take care of you... No one will get to you, i love you lovely heart... You are me i take care of you just the two of us i love you my big fat heart..."

i remember you flopped your hands, one two, over your own, newly discovered heart. How sweet. You felt it knocking back at you and were relieved.

"This is your inside," you said. Sort of. Your words were still unformed, like raw fudge, and they ran down your chin. You tried again, scooping them into passable forms. But the woman didn't respond. She just kept massaging. Maybe she was part of the herd after all. A straggler? A jet of blood shot up between her fingers, landing near your foot. Swooping down from branches overhead, three small, black birds began pecking furiously at the blood offering. That didn't seem right.

"Should you really have that out?" you asked. "Outside?" You took a step forward, pinching your nose against the smell. Up close, you could see the heart was covered in flies. That definitely didn't seem right.

"Says the one holding nose!" The woman suddenly cried. The flies nearest her face lifted cautiously, before settling again. *There's meat rotting on the shelves. Refugees starving in camps, and we can't keep up with our own butchers.* The before-words rush through you with a wave of nausea. You fought to concentrate on the heart, on the clearing.

"You want some things inside and some things outside," the woman was saying. "It's never enough, never enough for you."

"I was never enough for you."

96

"Don't be stupid Mariana. This is not about enough, this is about survival. Sign the form. They can get us out."

"There is no 'out', Bea."

These before-voices cut through you like a singing saw. Your stomach unspooled and you zipped up your anus tight to stop it all falling out. You staggered to the side, finding an edge, a tree trunk to lean on. It seemed to pulse under your hand.

"Mariana..." you slurred.

The woman stayed hidden behind her heart. "In, out; inout. Same."

If that were true, you could find the Mariana in your head, but out here, with your body. You remembered the herd kneading you, the difference between your skin and theirs. That was outside and inside you had organs *GLORIOUS ORGANS*. You breathed heavily but the air was the same temperature outside as in. It didn't feel like you were breathing at all. The woman pressed her cheek into the heart, softly stroking its quivering side. It seemed upset by the conversation.

You tried again to explain, watching the flies crawling over the giant organ. "This body is mine. It is not yours because of skin. You have yours and I have mine."

The woman's arm shot out, fist closed. She wound it in, popped a fly into her mouth. "You're not separate from me or from fly or from tree or from heart." She squeezed the heart on both sides and it gave off a little sigh, like a dormouse getting comfortable. "Heart sometimes in. Sometimes out. Sometimes i go in. Like this with bloodbitch—to join and open." She pushed her eyes halfway into the oozing flesh of the heart as if to say, *Right?* and it seemed to nod.

Releasing it, she turned to you. Stepping round the heart, she slumped over on bandy legs. You saw she had a high forehead and a straight thin nose *She could be quite pretty, if she made a bit of an effort.* She was covered in blood spatters, like a full-body tattoo, and then she was on you, touching you, wrapping herself around you.

"See, you're not whole, not walled-in not protected from anything outside everything moves freely—you're full of holes, see?" She was everywhere at once, working your mouth open and shoving her hand and arm deep down your throat. "It's all connected it's all inside and outside," and her hand emerged out of your *How well do you know your pussy? 10 things HE can do to make YOU go crazy.* She gave you a little tickle and you squirmed like *slinky.*

"You are tunnel," she said flatly. She withdrew her arm and gave it a good lick before waddling back to the heart, which rippled all over. The trio of birds settled on it and picked at it with their beaks. She gave them a half-hearted shoo and they lifted as though pulled from above, rising into the red canopy.

"Know heart inout. You keep them separate; you have things inside you do not know. There's a Who howling around inside you like a great wind."

You remembered the bodies on the beach and something slid down your throat. "My loss-I-don't-know-what?"

Bloodbitch shrugged. "Who. Chained banshee. Howling inside body." She looked at you over her thin nose. "You must bring her out and face her calmly." She had become strangely articulate. "With love."

Your chest pulled in tight like a drawstring. "How do you know my loss-I-don't-know-what. My Who?"

But she had turned from you, back to her enormous throbbing heart.

"How can I know?" you asked louder. "Maybe... Maybe you can bring out my Who and we can know it together?" You craned over to try and catch her eye.

She kept her back to you. "You want to know about together you go to moonlover or shrimpqueen. They're into that sort of thing."

shrimpqueen

"You're good at that, aren't you?"
"Good at what?"
"Leaving people behind."

You tried to hold onto what bloodbitch said but it wouldn't stick, the before-voices greasing your hollowed-out head.

You moved from the undergrowth into a cool woods, the heat thinning out. The scratching thicket elongated out into tall, thick trees, whose canopies rustled together in a humid sky-carpet way above in the dark-up. Their trunks were covered with a fine, glowing moss; you pushed a finger in and it bounced right back. Rejected. *How do the herd do it?*

You gave the tree a little pat and toddled off down a soft path that carved its way through the forest. Your movement was easier now, but not yet automatic. You had to think each muscle, every tendon and ligament and cell as you walked. *All 206 bones.*

"How will they get it in there? Just carve you open?"
"Yes Mariana, with a butcher's knife. No, it's just a small incision."
"Inside your skull."
"Only just inside."

You caught the tail of this before-voice. The Who inside of you stopped her howling and listened.

"What are they even putting in you?"
"Some bionic chip. To adjust to space, I guess. And it's got a bit of data storage."
"Upping your RAM."
"Apparently it's a security thing. Encryption."

"Bea!" A slammed drawer. "Listen to yourself. You have no idea. You're just going to let them shoot you up there. With a cracked skull. What about ... the pressure? Your head will literally explode."

"Will you just please sign your form so I can take it in tomorrow? There's not many spaces left and I want us on the same ship."

"..."

Something warm and wet in your arms. A teary face.

"Don't worry, they'll re-fuse our skulls. They won't explode."

The voices dissipated but the word *fused* remained.

You stopped walking and clutched your head, bending your knees. Was this what bloodbitch was talking about?

You ran your hands over, checking for gaps. Inside and outside must be connected. Inout. Open. You couldn't feel any gaps, oh *god* you *were* fused. The pressure of the howling Who, how would she get out? How would you bring her out? You pushed your numb hands over your head again and again, but there was nothing, nothing but your smooth, bald head.

You snapped up. *I have brown hair and green eyes—*

You used to have hair. Before you washed up. And now it was just a gap, or a mass of tendrilled gaps in the universe where your *hair* should be. You groaned, the pain flaring again. *It's the Who. She needs to be inside and out.* The howling was building. It pounded on the walls of your new bod.

Where was Mariana? She was in the before and the now. *She'll be able to extract my Who.* You gave the forest a meek smile. *Maybe even find my hair. Maybe she knows who Bea is.*

You moved along, clutching your belly, through the thin shafts of light that cut between the trees. Lapping through the broken fragments of the before were the noises of the forest. Chirps and long wails, calls and bells. You didn't know what they meant either, but they were softer listening and you tried to retune to the exterior panoply.

As you walked through the trees, shapes began popping up amongst them, objects that glowed with familiarity. Flotsam and jetsam from the before. Huge, big enough to step inside, with tubular bodies and pointed tops. *Aluminium alloy, fibre optic* now twisted into the bark of the trees. Swallowed up. *You recognised Arizona, Pyongyang, bad egg Kimmy.* No, not quite.

You stepped from the path and through mushy mire towards them. It was hard to see the objects all at once they were so massive. You reached out to tap one and it gave a hollow *bong. Bunker, Fat Man, Grave of the Fireflies.* You flipped through search results, nononononono, spinning a dance around the blunt truth of these cone-like structures. It was another gap, too big to hold in one place, at one time.

"I can't believe you believe this nuclear stuff Bea. It's so lazy."

"I don't care how they spin it Mariana. Bombs, civil war, the four horses themselves; we're being offered free passage! The seas are too slow. No one is listening to them."

"That's the problem."

"Don't be so childish. Would you rather be left behind? On a dying planet?"

"Everything's dying Bea, that's no reason to give up on life."

It's too much. Too movie-line. There's silence. Then, laughter.

"I've changed my mind; you can stay here."

"Thank god. I don't want to be stuck in a space tube with you anyway."

The giggles seemed to radiate out of your head and bounce around the trees like a windchime. A travelling wind snatched some up but a couple floated into the one of the huge cone cylinders. It echoed. There was movement from inside them; you felt it on your skin. Like when you hold your hands near together and feel the heat of one on the palm of the other.

Except this was skins; many, many face-skins. Appearing in the holes of these massive *ballistic missiles.* You brightened at finding the word. Although they were not these *ballistic missiles* anymore. Now, they were *home.*

More faces popped up. They were a thin, translucent brown, so different from the thick skins of the massaging herd and meaty muscle of the heart. Atop each small, bouncy head twirled a smoke of hair. *How come they got to keep theirs?*

"Intruder!" one of them cheeped.

Another one squawked: "Protect the queen." They seemed to float independently, like balloons, but then you noticed thin, string-like necks leading back to bodies still obscured by the *ballistic missile.*

Say cheese! Something told you to smile but the balloon heads shrieked and their bobbing grew more violent. "Protect the queen!"

You recoiled but they started pelting you with something small and hard, bruising your new skin. You ducked and dodged, looking like the *tube man outside the Tesla dealership.*

"Please," you said. "I need help. I need to release my Who, my inside banshee. I think she ate my hair and she hurts my tummy!"

The faces began to clench and puff, moving towards you, pouring out of the *ballistic missiles* like candy floss. You fell back. They dragged something up from the metal tube. First a leg appeared. The ankle was puffy and swollen and the *coughs* was wide open *I can show you the wooorld* and then she appeared, sliding out of her house *Aragog*; beast-woman.

She looked like nothing else you had met. She had multiple swollen bellies like a bunch of grapes; ten, twenty, more. Around her, the faces pulled their short, stumpy bodies, crowding their queen (presumably) and cooing softly.

"Move! Let me see her!" The queen shooed her attendants into the moss, but they wriggled up into the dangling vines and branches instead, hanging round her like a cloud.

She looked at you, struggling to catch her breath. Her face was red and flabby, edged with a short, white beard. Her two arms fluttered over her bellies. "You have something howling inside of you?"

"Yes. I have a Who inside of me and I don't know how to get her out."

102

The woman gasped. "i have many howls inside of me. Why won't they get out. GET OUT GET OUT GET OUT."

The balloon heads fussed around her. "Our spawn will come soon."

"Not long now, moontide grows strong."

"It calls them, our queen." They rubbed their cheeks against her swollen bellies.

Queen Bee. Big Momma. You moved nearer. "The moontide? This will release your howls, your banshees?"

"THEY ARE NOT BANSHEES," her drones roared in unison, snapping their faces round to you.

"Kin-brood crawl from womb, blood-plump. Not banshees," one hissed. It turned back to the translucent bump skin, grazing stubby fingertips across it.

The queen spoke quietly through the sheet of sweat on her face. "They *are* fat puppy-dogs of love and guts when they crawl from womb. But they are also whistling wind." She flicked her fingers to the sky. "Up, screams go. But not banshees."

Your stomach churned and you gasped with the pain. It was getting stronger.

"So, my banshee... She will crawl out too? Fat and gutsy? Another skin? Different from me?"

The queen eyed you. "No. Same but another. Your cores hold hands at the start, but then it is written in blood. Your sameness." She let out a sharp breath. "But you are strange creature. Mariana was right." Your ears pricked at this. "Bitty. You don't know who you are, so how will spawn know?"

"My loss-I-don't-know-what."

"i don't know how solid your howls will become, what you will spawn. A banshee is a howl of death. And how can that be new life?"

The women rubbed her many bellies, each humming in a different pitch like crystal glasses rimmed with sucked fingers, a xylophone of dinner party spit. Her attendants began to hum as well, swirling around in a frenzy. "Oh, they come soon!"

You spoke louder, over the sound of singing glass. "You know Mariana? Do you know where I can find her?"

A balloon head gnashed towards you. "Leave now! Brood come!" You stumbled back onto the glowing moss.

The queen gasped. "Find the bunnywomen. They draw things out."

You bolted into the ink.

moonlover

A white, plastic room.

"This is where we make the incision. After the transplant has been made, you'll feel a little out of sorts."

"Considering we'll be in a tube leaving Earth, I imagine we will feel a little strange."

Smiley face laughing, busying around your head. "A little nausea. Perhaps some short-term memory loss. We?"

"My girlfriend and I."

"Is she here as well?"

"Not today, she's having a harder time adjusting to the idea." More people enter the room.

"That's... unfortunate."

"She'll come around."

"I'm afraid the transplant will take place today, Bea."

They strap you in.

"What?"

"You'll be launched this evening."

"What? No, I'm not ready. I need my... my things. What about Mariana? We need to be on the same ship."

"I'm sure she'll get a later one. Now, please try to relax—"

"No, please wait! Mariana!"

You held Bea's words for as long as you could, your mouth echoing her words. *Mariana.*

At the edge of the forest, warm and cool air met like two dancers. In their between, larvae formed and ants argued. Atop an old car burying its face into a tree trunk, a clump of snails rolled in ecstasy. You passed through this shimmer, only feeling the cold.

You emerged out onto a cliff overlooking the black beach, now baked in moonlight. The corpses seemed part of the landscape now, rising dunes of the dark sand, their outlines blurred by the rustle of feeding. That seemed like a lifetime ago, yet you still felt the writhing on your skin. You traced their horizons in the air. Your Who whistled as a wind rushed by, late for work out at sea.

The whistle continued around you. *Inout.* You listened and its pitch dropped to a rumble. Turning, you saw a woman squatting on the balls of her feet. You were relieved to see just one belly and not swollen but nice and flat *101 tips to achieve your dream beach bod.* You shook your head. (The flashes still came but you barely felt them now. Look at me, i've even climbed inside of brackets to help out. We're getting there—soon you won't be able to tell the difference between us.)

She was crouched low, her *coughs* almost grazing the grass. All along her body were thick white stripes, one line down each arm and leg and her face glowed fluorescent white.

"Are you the bunnywomen?" you asked.

"Bunnywomen?" said the woman. "At the lake by now. With the bigblues. Oh yes, those big blue girls get pretty sick from that lake." You didn't know what she was talking about. Looking closer, you saw her eye sockets were empty, dark craters.

Your stomach groaned and you crouched to ease the pain. "My eyes used to be turned in too, but I turned them outward and now I can see. I see lots of things but I don't like to see the herd feed, they are feeding on my loss-I-don't-know-what. Do you feed?"

The painted lady laughed. "Yeah, i feed the girl." She gestures downward and you see her *coughs* really is grazing *free-grazing beef—you can* taste *the difference.* "And eyes are not turned in. On moon." She started jumping, springing around the clifftop meadow. She circled you, dancing and flicking her limbs towards the sky. "i know you." She smiled. "You one of the old ones."

You looked down at the mounds on the beach. *No, not one of* them. *Lying, rotting, stinking; fed on.* Your belly-pain throbbed. It didn't feel like you had a whole lot of time. Like, if the time between each throb of pain got shorter and shorter, then there would be no time left. Time was in your body now.

"Do you know where Mariana is?"

"Yup, you washed up on beach with head full of code, didn't you. Just like mariana said."

"Please, I am in pain. I need to find her. I think she knows my Who."

"i have heard of your who. i saw your corpses on the beach. i would be howling too if all my people were dead."

You recoiled. *Dead, dead, dead, dead.* The holes in her face glistened black.

"Where is Mariana?" you tried one last time.

"My howls come from moon." She smiled dreamily, her dancing making her shift and slip in the moonlight. "i call to her, gust-gluttals to whistling ribbons and she hears me. She pulls the stomachs out and round. Then kin-brood crawl out of woods." She hooked a finger back in the direction of the trees.

You shook your head. No. No more. No more moon-children or strange-women, you wanted Mariana. You wanted the pain to stop. You turned away from her *You're good at that aren't you* and began to run.

"Running away isn't the answer, Bea."
"We don't have much time."

As you ran, you started to sob. Your limbs hot with run, your face hot with tears. Your head bald as a baby's.

"It's only going to get worse, Mariana."
"We're needed here."
"There's nothing left here!"
"What about everyone left behind? Everyone who wasn't selected for Golden Disc?"

The voices pound in; they throb in time with the pain in your stomach. Who. Who. Who.

"They can't take everyone."
"And why you Bea? Who are you?"

You ran blind. Away from the stinking bodies. Away from the babes in the wood. The grass underfoot became hard, then loosened into single rocks, which cackled beneath you. The ground sloped upwards and you climbed higher through the dark. Your bare feet were hot on cold rock *Shoes, where are my shoes?* The winds buffed you and for the first time you realised, crawling and yapping in the night, that you were completely naked. *In the buff.*

Your hands clasped at thin air. There were no more rocks above you. You were at the top. *Not a stitch to clothe nor fire to warm me.* Just you, jutting out one-woman against the chasm-dark sky. That's how i first saw you. i was so close now.

You wiped your snotty nose and gazed back down the slope's darkness, finding the humming outline of the woods and the bared teeth of the cliff edge. You wrapped your arms tight around your chest and crouched low on the ground, the earth inside you pulling you down like a magnet. *Like the moon,* you sneered through a hiccup.

Beneath you, a pair of centipedes reared up to give thanks to the heavenly object.

You heard a splash somewhere off in the world. You jumped up, choking, stumbled on the rocky edge. Something had turned in you. Your Who had made you more wary. You had an impulse to protect. The dark holes of the moonlover's eyes. The snarling of the shrimpqueen's drones. You clutched your swelling stomach. i was not far off.

You turned away from the slope. The ground ahead was flat and uniform. A metallic tang pinched the air. You unfurled a leg like a tentacle and dipped a toe. Water. You were standing at the foot of a huge, black lake.

Another splash. Bubbles drifted towards you; something was coming to surface. A smooth bump grew from the water. A head. Bald as yours but enormous and lumbering, eyes closed half-moon against swollen cheeks. It was a woman... Sort of. She was huge. Her form, glittering and dark blue, rose out from the water, puffing out jets of steam. Suddenly, with a great spurt of water, another surfaced behind her. You stood, bound tightly with fear, as they waded slowly out of the water, moving off to the shallows at the side. A procession of giants.

Their speed calmed you a little. Their movements had purpose, a measured quality that dampened the sharp moans of the howling Who. They knew where they were going. They probably knew who they were. You picked your way after them.

They reached the edge of a tree line and began to weave into the woods. These weren't carpeted moss like the first forest—the trees here protruded from the flaky and cracked earth like bones. Yours echoed in response as you moved through them.

You followed the giants to a clearing, stopping behind a tree. You watched them stop one by one, forming a V shape in rows. The pain was near wrenching you in two.

As though reflections of the tree's themselves, three long, sinewy figures emerged. Their white heads were elongated and split into two thick horns. Their eyes were glassy, like geometric prisms, a red scratch of a pupil darting around inside. *The bunnywomen.*

Squatting next to them was a figure, more your size. Its head was bowed. It was muttering.

The bloated blue creature at the front of the line flopped on her side with a crash that shook the earth, rolling over to reveal her pale belly with a groan. You clung on to the slip of trunk. The bunnywomen moved forwards and began to pick things off her, little parasitic wriggles. When they sliced her open you gasped in mirrored pain and watched as they extracted what looked like a hard, fatty lump.

There was a breath's moment. A blood-plump bat swooped by from the beach, filled with human.

Whilst the huge creature clambered to her feet, the bunnywomen stuffed the lump into their mouths, sucking and burping down the offending tumour. That creaking blubber of blue moved off, and the next moved in to take her place.

You watched this, horrified. This was just like the bodies on the beach. Was nothing sacred?

"Everyone will turn on each other. It'll be like Mad Max. Do you want to be in Mad Max, Mariana?"

"I'd rather be in Mad Max than 2001."

This is what made you different to these people. A sense of deference to each other, a respect of the distance. Not gorging on their corpses or feeding on their cancerous lumps. You backed away, shaking your head, and clutching your belly. The Who, it was coming, i was coming now. You fell onto the hard ground. You saw the shorter figure move towards you, but it was only as her palm flattened against your shoulder that you recognised her.

"Mariana!" you roared, thrashing on the dead, cracked soil. Your mouth fizzed, eyes rolling wildly.

"i'm here," said mariana, one hand gripping yours, another mopping your sweaty, bald brow.

"She's coming," you cried. "My Who, she's coming."

"i know, i know," she soothed.

"You'll leave without me. Us."

You raised your eyes to meet mariana's.

"They're flying people off the fucking planet! You're coming with me, Mariana."

Locked into her gaze you felt the Who claw and scream inside.

"No, Bea."

Mariana knew, she was part of it, your loss-you-don't-know-what.

"I'm going to stay. I'm going to help."

You widened your eyes and with a deafening flash, you lost consciousness.

Under the watch of the moon and the insects and the seagarbage gull, they worked quickly. Mariana parted your legs and saw what her dirt had made. The herd rubbed your swollen belly and a sound like singing glass rang out across the acrid lake.

110

In her cave, bloodbitch whispered to her heart, "Inside, outside, inout."

The moonlover on the cliff called gust-gluttals to whistling ribbons. She called it forth.

Mariana reached in but it was a vicious thing, clinging to you. You were half gone, me taking your place. We sobbed together. Then the bunnywomen sliced and it was free and it was coming out.

We screamed as they dragged out something thin and dribbly from inside of us, drenched in electric mucus. Mariana held it up to the moon's light and the mucus slid down her arms. The thing had a pulsing red light and rows of tiny shark teeth. We looked at it, you and me together, you the old, and me, the burgeoning new.

This is what you spawned. i looked away as they drowned it in the lake.

i was not you anymore.

Coming to in the woods, i felt clogged and blurry. Mariana knelt in front of me, palms on the earth. Around her crouched the herd. Anemone eyes and arched nose. Multi-tongue flicking my arm.

i sat up too quickly, clacking my hands between my legs but they closed on nothing.

"Where's my Who?" i croaked.

"You?" said mariana. "We drowned that thing in the lake. It's gone now."

"Along with the feast," multi-tongue grumbled. There was blood all around her mouth.

i cradled my head. Listened for the voices. "Where have they gone? Where's Bea?"

Mariana smiled. "But you are still bea."

"I... Bea was the last one! The last human, washed up."

Anemone-eyes gave a screech of laughter. Mariana rubbed my bald head like a lamp. "Honey, there have been hundreds like us. Washing up all over. You really thought you were the only one?"

i took mariana's hand. "They did the transplant before i could find you. i left you behind."

Mariana brought my foot to her face. "i was right behind you. My tube crashed back down not long before yours did. i don't know how long we were gone." The sun was breaking over the mountain.

i bit my lip. "Where are we?"

"Lay down," mariana said, taking a long thread of twisted green vines from arched nose. "Us-we will sew you up. Tell you everything we know."

THE ENDLING

I was nine when my mother told me of The Endling.

She perched on the end of my bed with her face threaded with a suspense so taut I was sure she believed in her too. With little claw-like fingers, she enacted her prowling of the city's deserted streets. At the sleepovers, me and the other girls shared our findings.

"My mum told me she has black stripes across her ribs," said Sweetums. "And huge sharp teeth!"

"Nu-uh," disagreed Honeybear. "My mum said she has a fat arse," she dropped her fingertips to the floor in front of her, sticking her bottom high in the air, to a chorus of high-pitched shrieks and giggles, "with thick, black feathers like smoke sprouting from her bumhole." She stepped around the bunker like this, wiggling her behind back and forth. We heard snorts from the corner, and whipped our heads round to glare at the mums huddled in the shadows, passing a cup of weak tea between them. "Sorry, sorry," they waved their tea-free hands.

"Well, *my* mum," Darling leaned forward to bring the attention back to the centre, "says The Endling has tusks as heavy as time itself," she held her arms out in front of her, shoulders hunched close to her face. She swung them near Sweetums, and Sweetums fell back onto her sleeping mat with a crinkled face and the usual: "Stop iiiiiiiit!"

"How can *time* be heavy?" asked Honeybear. "We can't even see it. It's just there—" she spread her fingers out wide in front of her, palms up, "—and then it's gone!" She clapped her hands together.

"I think Darling means the unbearable dragging of days, which The Endling feels so much more because she's all alone," said Dear in her voice like stone. The younger girls went quiet. Dear continued. "She is the most precious, and yet, without another, she is worthless. She wanders the ashes searching for her mate, unaware that she's the only one left. Her solitude is what creates her, and destroys her, each day."

I gave Dear a look; we were about the same age and she should know better. Everything had grown so silent we could hear the mums shuffling and whispering in their corner, but we ignored them as best we could. They promised we could carry on having sleepovers like before, and them huddling in the corner was the best we could do now that all of us gals were stuck down in this bunker together. Sweetums started to cry.

I reached out a hand and took Dear's cold one, and with my other hand wrangled Honeybear's still. We formed a seated circle. "Well," I began, "my mum told me The Endling's loneliness means that she has crossed eyes, which have turned to each other for company," (Honeybear pulled a face for Sweetums beside her and Sweetums giggled through her tears) "and her voice has retreated inside her head."

"No one to tell her stories?" asked Darling.

I glanced up. I couldn't pick out my own mum from the gaggle but I knew she was among them, listening.

"She tells *herself* stories whilst she patrols the city," I say. "She dreams of finding girls in bunkers—" Sweetums whimpered, but I met her fearful eyes, "—and bringing them news of what she has seen."

ACKNOWLEDGEMENTS

Like the composite bodies of all things, this collection has only been possible due to the collaborative help and support of many different people. Obviously, without my wonderful colleague and friend Lexie Angelo, and her indefatigable creative and entrepreneurial spirit and energy that have made Radical Bookshop possible, these stories would still be yapping about in my hard drive. Thank you for publishing this collection and sorry the edits dragged on. Thanks to the Creative Writing Programme at The University of Edinburgh, for the space to write; to my workshop group for invaluable community, habit, and commitment building; and to Jane McKie, for seeing my strange thoughts as they were meant to be seen. To all those that read and gave edits; Jack, Bonnie. Thank you to my teachers and mentors over the years, especially those at Penrice; to Mr Jackson, who told me to 'use my writing to change the world' (bit ambitious) and Ryan Monger for modelling the rebellious creative spirit. To my incredible friends and family; to Mono, for your belief; to Mum, for your imagination, humour, and storytelling gifts; to Laurence, for your ferocity. To my Dad, who died a while ago but still makes me laugh. Lastly, to Bleg, who read countless versions, gave unending suggestions, was unfalteringly silly and generally loved the stories, and me.

ABOUT THE AUTHOR

Sam Le Butt is a writer based in Bristol, UK. After completing her Creative Writing Masters at the University of Edinburgh, she is now pursuing her English Literature PhD in monstrous bodies in contemporary eco narratives. She worked as the Chief Editor and writing mentor for The Selkie literary magazine and has taught English in Japan and the UK. Her short fiction can be found in various anthologies, and she is working on her first novel, set in a darkly comic environmental dystopia.